D1528996

1

This book is dedicated to Angela Taylor and Ann West. Continue to S.I.P....

Introduction…

If you love a motherfucka enough, you'll lie to yourself. You won't need their lies. You'll create your own. You'll become blind to the truth because you only want to see the fantasy that you've created in your mind. I'm not talking about no regular love. I'm talking about that cloud nine type of love that has you feeling like you're the only two in the world who exist, when you're together. I'm talking about the type of love that goes way beyond the physical, where you feel mentally and spiritually connected. That's the kind of love, I'm talking about… Have you ever experienced that type of love?

A Toxic Luv Story (Choc and Yaya) By La'Tonya West

Good Morning

The room smelled of Black Love incense and vanilla bean scented candles, as R. Kelly's song _Get Up On A Room_ spilled from the speakers, on repeat. It was a little past five in the morning, and Choc and Yaya were on their third round. This was the second time; he'd woken her from her sleep in the past two hours.

"Tell me, you love me." Choc whispered in Yaya's ear, while stroking her nice and slowly. He licked her ear, before sucking on her earlobe.

Wrapping her legs around his waist, Yaya moaned. "I love you, Choc. Oh god, I love you." She meant those words from the depths of her soul. She'd never said those words to anyone else and meant them as much as she did when saying them to Choc. Honestly, _I love you_ didn't even come close to describing the way she felt about him. It was way more intense than love. It was indescribable.

"Promise me that no matter what, you're going to be mine forever." He kissed her, going deeper with each stroke but keeping the same rhythm. He didn't want to rush this moment. He wanted to take his time with her and make love to her, like he'd never done before. He wanted this time to play over and over in her head, every time that she thought of him. Not just the love making but the things that he was asking her to say.

"I promise."

"You promise, what?" He thrust into her, hard and deep.

"Oh shit!" Yaya squealed, her body shivering beneath him. "Fuck! Why do you have to feel so good?"

He withdrew himself, before thrusting into her, hard and deep again. "You promise what?"

On the brink of cumming, she wrapped her legs around him tighter, her hands were on his back, her fingertips pressing into his skin, trying to pull him deeper inside her. "I promise, I'll be yours forever."

"You mean it?" He asked, kissing her lips.

"Yes…I mean it." She moaned, between kisses.

"You better." He threatened, still kissing her. He picked up his pace just a little, as he felt her becoming wetter and his orgasm building. He wasn't sure if he'd be able to hold it much longer. "I love you, too, Yaya. You know that don't you?"

"Yes, I know."

"Good. Now, go ahead and cum on this dick. So, I can cum with you." Kissing her passionately, he stroked in and out of her. A man on a mission and it wasn't long

7

before her body began to convulse beneath him, letting him know that his mission had been accomplished. Which let him know that it was okay to release his own orgasm. He released what felt like buckets of semen inside of her, flooding her insides. His orgasm was so intense that his toes curled and popped. He even felt lightheaded. "Gotdamn! Fuck!"

Yaya lay beneath him, still riding the waves of her own orgasm, and wishing that he could stay inside of her forever. She loved the feeling of them being connected. No man had ever come close to making her feel the way that Choc did. She had never experienced emotions so strong for any of her boyfriends in the past. That is why she was confident that he was her soulmate.

Choc kissed her neck. "I have to go, beautiful." He tried to get up, but she locked her legs and arms around him.

"Can't you just call out today?" She whined, hating to see him go.

"I wish, I could but I've gotta go chase this bag." He kissed her, again. She sucked on his bottom lip and then opened her mouth just a little, inviting his tongue inside. He gladly accepted the invitation. Their tongues intertwined, doing a slow dance. She kissed him with so much passion.

He felt his manhood trying to come to life, again. It was as if, she was making love to him with her mouth. He pulled away, whispering. "Baby, I have to go." He really needed to go and if he stayed there inside of her any longer. He knew they would no doubt embark on round four.

Reluctantly, Yaya unlocked her legs, releasing him. "Okay." She pouted.

Choc got up and then leaned down and gave her a quick peck. "I love your spoiled ass." He chuckled.

"How am I spoiled, if I never get my way?" Yaya questioned, continuing to pout.

"Oh, you get your way. Just not as much as you would like." He replied.

"Whatever." She retorted, flipping over on her stomach and getting comfortable.

"*Whatever.*" Choc mumbled in a mocking tone and then smacked her on the butt. Before, turning and leaving the room. He went down the hall to the bathroom and washed up. When he was done, he went back in the bedroom and got dressed. By now, Yaya had dozed off and was snoring softly. He smirked to himself, knowing he'd worn her out. He got a kick out of fucking her to sleep. He walked over to the bed and shook her, gently. "Ya, wake up. I'm about to leave."

Her eyes fluttered open. "Huh?"

"I said, I'm about to go. Get up and walk me to the door."

"Choc, just lock the door on your way out."

"Nah, I want you to walk me out. Come on." He reached down and pulled the covers off her. Knowing that would get her up.

Smacking her lips, she pushed herself up with her arms and got up. She sat on the side of the bed, cursing him in her head. She was grumpy because he'd kept her up most of the night and now, he still wouldn't allow her to get any rest. "Why are you so dag on worrisome? You know good and well that you've been locking that door when you leave. Now, this morning you need me to walk you to the door." She grumbled, getting up, while adjusting the little night gown that she was wearing.

Choc ignored her little attitude and kissed her, again. "Hush that noise and come on, woman." He held out his hand.

"What?" Yaya questioned.

"Give me, your hand."

"Choc, I don't know what you want or what you've done but you sure have been extremely nice for the past month or so." She said, placing her hand in his.

"I haven't done anything. I just be wanting you to know, I love you. So, I've been trying to show that more." He replied, as they walked down the hallway towards the front door.

Yaya blushed because he had been doing a lot better. "I appreciate it, baby. Now, if you could just learn how to reply back when I text you or just shoot me a text throughout the day to let me know you're good. I'd really appreciate that."

"I will." He told her as they reached the door. He turned and pulled her into his arms, hugging her tightly. "I love you, Ya."

"I love you, too, baby." She looked up at him and he kissed her, again. A weird feeling formed in the pit of her stomach. His behavior was telling her that something wasn't right, but she brushed the feeling off and decided not to speak on it. He was doing good, and she didn't want to ruin it by pestering him about his reasons why. This is what she'd been wanting. Things weren't perfect between them, but they were better. So, she was just going to accept that and enjoy it while it lasted.

"Alright. I've gotta get out of here." Choc let her know, breaking their embrace. "Lock the door and go get some rest."

"Alright. Are you coming back tonight?"

He opened the door, without looking back and called over his shoulder. "Maybe."

"Okay. Well, drive safely and I love you." Yaya called after him. She was disappointed in the answer he'd just given, but tried not to let it show.

Stopping on the porch, Choc finally looked back. "I love you, too." Then, he continued to his car, got in, and left.

Yaya locked the door and headed back to bed.

Yaya

"Feelings, so deep in my feelings. No, this ain't really like me. Can't control my anxiety. Feeling, like I'm touching the ceiling. When I'm with you, I can't breathe. Boy, you do something to me." My homegirl, Keema and I, sang at the top of our lungs.

It was Friday night and the two of us were at my place. She was seated in front of my vanity mirror, putting the finishing touches on her makeup. While, I sat on the bed having a glass of wine and watching her two-year-old son DJ play with toys. That was the reason she'd come over after work. So, that she'd have someone to keep an eye on DJ, while she got dressed for her date. I didn't mind. This was something we did all the time. I actually enjoyed watching him for her. I was glad I could help her out. My sister, Mari, was a single mom. So, I knew firsthand how hard it could be to get a minute to yourself, from watching her with my nephew.

Keema and I worked together, which is how we met. We were both hair stylists at Posh, located in my hometown of Boykins, VA, minutes away from the North Carolina state line. The fact that we were so close to the state line worked in our favor. Clients from both North Carolina and Virginia poured into our spot on a daily basis, keeping us super busy. Posh was just as popular today as it had been twelve years, ago. When it first opened for business. I'd been at Posh now for a little over ten years. We had some of the best stylists and the thing I liked most about working there was the owner Judy was always pushing for us to further our education. We often frequented hair shows and different cosmetology classes, learning new techniques. I was a loctician, specializing in locs. Learning how to style, take care of, and repair them. I absolutely loved what I did. So much so that I accepted clients at my home after business hours and on my days off. I did other things besides locs but they were my specialty.

Keema was originally from Roanoke Rapids, North Carolina, which is thirty-five minutes from Boykins. She'd recently moved back to Boykins and joined the Posh family a little over two years ago. She and I hit it off, instantly. Once, she told me who her relatives were. I knew her family really well because I used to date her cousin. I loved her family, and they loved me. We went way back. Till this day, they still showed me love whenever they saw me. They were like my extended family. I had a lot of love and respect for them. So, I kinda felt as if it was my job to look after and help Keema in any way I could. She was eight years younger than me and sometimes that made our friendship a little stressful because in some ways she was still very immature.

When the song went off, I called for *Alexa* to turn down the volume on my Echo Dot. "Girl, he is so freakin cute!" I gushed, admiring DJ. "He got me wanting to toss my birth control pills in the trash and gone let Choc put a baby in me!"

Keema stopped applying her eyelash to look at me. "Bitch, you must have some coke mixed in that Moscato." She rolled her eyes and then smacked her lips, before adding, "Here you are thirty-seven with no kids, can come and go as you please, and you're talking about letting a nigga put a baby in you. Chile, it has to be drugs that got you saying some stupid shit like that."

"Damn, why I gotta be on drugs to want a baby? Choc and I would make some gorgeous chocolate babies." I blushed at the thought of my midnight chocolate obsession and I making some little chocolate babies that were a perfect mixture of the both of us. Recently, I'd been thinking about it constantly. Throughout the day, I often fantasized about being pregnant and having Choc pamper and spoil me while I carried our child. The thought of it made my heart swell. The amount of love I held in my heart for Choc was indescribable and nothing would've made me happier than having his baby.

"Girrrrrrl, you done lost it! You went from one baby to babies. Listen, I love DJ to death, and I would do anything for my baby, but I can't sit here and lie. I'm not one of those mothers who be saying I can't imagine my life without my baby. Shiiiid, I can. A bitch would be living my best fuckin life! I wouldn't have to wait on his triflin ass daddy to come pick him up. So, that I could have some time for myself. I could travel whenever I wanted to, sleep in late, and not have to worry about taking care of anyone but myself. I know, I probably sound fucked up but it's the truth. That nigga trapped me."

"Trapped you?" I questioned, looking at her wide eyed. I couldn't believe she felt this way but what was even more shocking is that she was actually admitting this to me.

"Hell yeah, he trapped me." She repeated. She paused for a second and finished applying her lash before turning to face me. "I told Dro, I didn't want any kids."

"So, how did he trap you?" I asked, confused.

"Because I can't take any kind of birth control. I've tried the pills. They made me sick as a dog. Every brand I tried. Then, I tried the shot. Again, I stayed sick. I even tried the IUD. That shit made me bleed so bad that I had to have it removed. Plus, I kept breaking out around the spot where they implanted it. So, I told him that he would have to use rubbers. Well, you know how that goes. A nigga always wanna feel it without the rubber. So, I told him to make sure that he pulled out. Needless to say, he didn't. Then, when I got pregnant and wanted to have an abortion, he lost it. He wanted to put hands on me. Then he told me, if I did it, he wouldn't ever fuck with me again in life. He begged and begged for me not to kill his baby. I ain't no cold-hearted bitch. I loved him at the time…let me rephrase that. I was in love with his black ass at the time. So, I gave in and gave him his son but honey, if I knew then what I know, now. I wouldn't have done it. I would've kept my freedom. Now look, me and that nigga ain't even together and I can barely stand his ass."

"Uh-ugh!" I threw up my hand in disbelief, while taking a sip from my wine glass. "Girl, you're trippin. You're blessed. There are people who can't even have babies and here you are with this adorable baby talking about you regret having him. I'm glad he can't understand what you're saying."

"Stop being so freakin dramatic, Yaya. I'm not saying I regret him. That's not the way, I mean it. All I'm

17

saying is, I'm not the maternal type. I could've been fine with not having children." Keema clarified, before turning around to finish what she was doing.

I decided to let it go. I didn't feel like going back and forth with her and this turning into something bigger than what it had to be. She felt how she felt and that was her business. "So, what time is Dro coming to pick up little man?"

"He's supposed to be here by 8:30." She replied, holding up her wrist and looking at her Apple watch. "It's ten past eight, now. He should be pulling up, soon."

"Oh ok." I looked back down at DJ. He was now stretched out on the floor with his sippy cup in his mouth, pulling on his ear. I got up, put my glass on the nightstand then reached down and picked him up. I sat back on the bed, rocking him slowly in my arms.

A few minutes later, Keema stood up and turned around. "So, how do I look?"

I looked up at her, taking in her full look, from the wet and wavy lacefront to the form fitting, thigh length dress she was wearing. "Girl, you already know you look good." I complimented her before asking. "What kind of shoes are you wearing?"

"Some lime green and black stilettos." She replied. Which wasn't surprising at all because she loved bright colors. Also, this made the lime green eyeshadow smeared above her eyes make sense. Moving her hair back from her face, she blinked. "How did I do on this beat?" She asked, referring to her makeup.

"You're getting better and better each time." I nodded, admiring how much her skills had progressed.

"Thank you, girly." She beamed. "I'm thinking about asking Judy if I can start doing makeup at the shop. It's just an idea I've been tossing around in my head, but I think it's a good idea. What do you think?"

"I think, you should, and I believe Judy would give you the ok to do it. It wouldn't hurt to ask. You could also do lashes, too. You would make a killing up in there. These women nowadays can't leave the house without a pair of lashes and a lot of them don't know how to apply them or aren't good at it. Like myself. Even though, I only wear them for special occasions. Anyways, I think you should go for it."

Keema nodded in agreement. "Yeah, I should. I'm going to holla at her about it Monday. Since, I won't be there tomorrow."

"Sounds like a plan."

Keema's phone and watch chimed and at the same time the doorbell rang. Looking at her watch, Keema announced. "Dro's here. Can you get the door? I need to try and lay the edges on this frontal again before Hakeem gets here."

"Yeah, I got it." Rising to my feet with DJ on my hip, I headed to the door. When I reached the door, I looked out through the peephole to make sure that it was Dro. After verifying that it was indeed him, I unlocked and opened the door. "Hey, come on in." I greeted him.

"What's up?" He replied and then turned his attention to DJ who was now wide awake. "What's up, lil man?"

"Daaaaaa!" DJ squealed, nearly jumping out of my arms.

Dro reached out and took him from me and I closed the door.

"Keema's down the hall in my room getting dressed. If you wanted to see her…I mean…I guess, she wants to speak to you before you take him." I rambled, feeling a little awkward. Keema should've been handling this because I wasn't sure of how they did things and after hearing how she felt about motherhood. I wasn't sure if she wanted to kiss her baby goodbye or not.

20

"Yeah, let me holla at her." Dro replied, finally tearing his attention away from DJ to look at me.

When he looked at me, I finally got a really good look at him. I'd seen him a few times but never up close. This was my first time being this close to him. He was fine as shit. This man exuded sex appeal. His midnight chocolate skin was smooth, not a blemish in sight. He had a close cut with waves deep enough to make a bitch seasick. By him having on short sleeves, I could see that both his arms were decorated with tattoos, along with his neck. He was a little on the thick side, not fat or chubby but he had some meat on his bones. Then, to top it all off, he had a nice smile.

Damn, he's fine! I thought to myself. Immediately feeling ashamed of my thoughts, I shook my head as if to shake my thoughts away. "You can follow me." I told him, leading the way to my bedroom.

When we entered the bedroom, Keema was still messing with the edges of her wig. She glanced up at us, through the mirror, before turning around. "Hey." She spoke, dryly to Dro.

"What's up?" He replied, returning the same dry energy.

Getting up from my vanity, Keema crossed the room to the loveseat in the corner of the room. Lifting the small spider man book bag, she said. "I put three outfits for him in his bag. He has a few Pull-Ups in there as well, but you will probably have to buy him some more because he goes through them fast as hell…"

"Why is he using the bathroom in his Pull-Ups instead of his potty?" Dro interrupted.

"Because he doesn't tell me when he has to go to the bathroom and by the time I check, he's already pissy or shitty." Keema snapped.

"Keema, you supposed to ask him or take him and sit him on the potty even when he says he doesn't have to go."

Keema rolled her eyes while smacking her lips. "So, you don't think I've been doing that?"

"You didn't just say you were doing that."

Waving her hand dismissively, Keema grabbed the rest of DJ's bags and shoved them in Dro's free arm. "Here! You can leave now because I do not have the time tuh-day. I have a date and you are not about to fuck up my mood, talking bout dumb shit. Just buy the fuckin Pull-Ups! The fuck? That's what they're for, him to piss and shit in."

Dro exploded. "That's your fuckin problem. The only thing you got time for is running the streets and chasing niggas, with that Halloween makeup all caked up on your fuckin face. Lookin like a fuckin joke. Take some time with your fuckin son! Potty training him ain't hard. You just got to make time."

"Boy, please get the fuck out because I ain't trying to hear none of that shit you talkin."

"You're a goofy ass bi..." He caught himself before letting the word bitch slip from his lips. "Yo, you really need to get your priorities straight and grow the fuck up. I'm tired of arguing with you and especially in front of my son. He deserves better than that from both of us but you're so selfish you can't put anyone else's needs before your own...not even the life you brought in this world. You're sad as fuck, for real."

"Only thing sad is you!" Keema accused. Then began to laugh, sticking her tongue out in a taunting manner. "I know why you're really mad. You really mad because I'm going out. Yeah, that's why you really mad. This ain't about no damn Pull-Ups."

"What?" He questioned, wearing a confused expression. "You're delusional as fuck, too. I ain't about to even keep going back and forth with you."

"Don't! It still doesn't change the fact that you're big mad!" She continued to laugh.

Dro looked at me and spoke. "I apologize for disrespecting your home, ma'am." Without another word, he walked out.

I followed him and locked the front door, once he had made it to his car with DJ.

"I swear, I can't stand his black ass!" Keema fumed, entering the living room, with her pocketbook on her shoulder, keys in one hand and an overnight bag in the other.

I shook my head before flopping down on the sofa. "Chile, y'all need to get it together. DJ doesn't need to be seeing the two of you going at it like that. That was too much."

"Girl, bye. Fuck that shit you're talking! His bitch ass daddy always coming for me like I don't know how to be a fuckin mom. If that's how he feels then why don't he take him and raise him. Then, I can have my fuckin life back. He was the one who wanted a baby not me! I do my fuckin best and it still ain't good enough."

Hearing her express it in that way, I felt bad for her because I understood feeling like you're doing your best and it's not appreciated or acknowledged. "Maybe once you guys have had a chance to cool off, the two of you can sit down and you can explain to him how you feel like you explained to me…minus the cursing. Maybe, he'll get a better understanding of how you feel and be less judgmental."

Sucking her teeth, she let her eyes roll up in her head. "Yaya, you really make my ass itch thinking you're Iyanla Vanzant. I don't need you to coach me on how to fix shit with Dro. I've been dealing with that nigga for over three years, now. I don't care how I explain or express shit to him. He's gonna respond in the same way. Like he knows every-fuckin-thing and like everything I do ain't good enough. That's always been our issue."

I threw up my hands in surrender. "Cool, you got it. That's y'all situation. So, I will keep my opinion to myself but just meet him at your house next time. So, I won't have to witness y'all drama. That way, I won't be trying to coach you on how to fix it or making your ass itch. How about that?" I'd had enough of her slick ass mouth for one night.

Cocking her head to one side, she asked. "So now, you in your feelings?" Before I could respond, she snapped. "You know what? I don't even give a damn at this point. I'm gone." She started towards the front door.

"Keema, no one is in their feelings but you. You're upset with Dro and taking it out on me. I was simply trying to give you some friendly advice because that's what friends do. You got smart with me."

She stopped and turned to face me. "I just feel like you always think you have the answers to everything but everybody ain't like you. I've been dealing with my baby daddy long enough to know how he is. You don't think, I've tried talking to Dro in every way to get him to understand how I feel. He thinks he knows everything and is better than everyone else. That shit's annoying. That's why I got smart with you." She paused and let out an exaggerated breath. "Listen, my bad. I shouldn't have taken it there with you. You're right, I am taking out my anger for Dro on you. I just really feel like no one understands me."

Not really wanting to discuss her baby daddy issues or anything else any longer, I decided to just drop it. There was really no need to take anything she said to heart, anyways. This wasn't anything new. This was typical Keema. She would get upset like this, blow up, and then call the next day apologizing. This is what I meant when I said she could be very immature at times. I did a good job of ignoring her tantrums, but I was growing tired of it. I wasn't sure of how many more tantrums I was gonna be able to deal with before falling back from her. I didn't have time for her childish behavior. Dro and everyone else could deal with it but Yaya was close to washing her hands of it. "I understand. We're good." I plastered on a fake smile, ready for her to leave.

"Alright. I'm gonna head on out, then. I'll call you tomorrow."

"Alright." I waved from the sofa.

She left and I got up and locked the door. Then, turned off all the lights in the front part of the house, before going back down the hall to my bedroom.

In the room, I took a seat on the edge of the bed and picked up my phone from the nightstand to check and see if Choc had called or text. Honestly, I knew without looking that he hadn't, but I was hoping that I was wrong. Looking down at my screen, what I already knew was confirmed. There wasn't anything from him. *I'm so sick of this shit.* I thought to myself. But was I really? Because I knew in my heart that the moment he called, texted, or came by, I was going to answer the phone or door. What the two of us shared could be better described as a situationship rather than a relationship. He walked in and out of my life whenever he felt like it and my dumb ass accepted it. It'd been that way for most of our relationship.

We'd been together now, for over three years and he still couldn't decide if I was the one. Whereas, I knew without a doubt that he was the one. I loved this man with everything in me and I prayed daily for him to love me back one day the same way I loved him…unconditionally. I accepted him as he was. He had more flaws than I could count, with the biggest one being his selfishness. However, I looked past it all because my heart kept telling me that all he needed was someone to love him correctly and not give up on him. From the stories that he'd shared with me about his past, I knew that he'd been through a lot. I figured, if I loved him enough and showed him that no matter what, I wasn't giving up on him. One day, he would finally see me and see that my love was pure and genuine.

My sister, parents, Keema and my other good friend, Ajah, told me constantly that I needed to cut all ties with Choc and move on but of course, I wasn't trying to hear what they were saying. They couldn't feel for me. They had no idea of how fearful I felt at the thought of him not being in my life. I couldn't imagine letting him go or more importantly having to see him get it right with someone else. The thought of that broke my heart. I'd rather accept him and all of the bullshit that came with him than lose him, completely. I had hope for him and I. When I envisioned my future, I saw him in it. I saw us happy. I saw us married with a family. I'm not sure if I was just fooling myself or if what I imagined was really possible, but I truly felt with every fiber of my being that it was. My heart told me that he was my soulmate. I'd never felt for anyone what I felt for him, and I just couldn't let go of that feeling. It wasn't about the sex or anything like that. I felt like, I connected with him on a spiritual level. Whatever, it was that had me feeling the way I did, I wasn't ready to walk away from it.

After sending Choc a text, asking where he was. I opened the Facebook app and scrolled for a minute. Then, checked Instagram. Not much was going on, on either app. So, I placed my phone back on the nightstand and decided to get ready for bed. I got up, went down the hall to the bathroom and took a shower. When I got out, I put on a sexy little night gown. Just in case, Choc showed up in the middle of the night. Then, I grabbed my wine glass from earlier and went into the kitchen to refill it. After getting my wine, I went back into my room, crawled into bed and checked my phone. Still nothing from Choc. I tried calling him, but his phone went straight to voicemail without even ringing. I tried again but the same thing happened. I went to my messages to send him another text, only to see that the last text didn't say delivered. *I know, he didn't block me.* I thought. My heart dropped to my stomach. I went back to Facebook and typed his name in the search bar. ChocSavage Branch. Nothing for him showed up. I went to Messenger and scrolled down to our messages. It no longer said his name. It now said Facebook User. Tears stung the backs of my eyes and seconds later, spilled down my cheeks. This had come out of nowhere. Everything had been fine when he'd left that morning. How had we gone from him making love to me all night and telling me how much he loved me to this? This wasn't making any sense! The feeling that I'd felt in the pit of my stomach that morning returned. I couldn't describe it, but it was an eerie feeling, like my body was trying to tell me something. Kinda like the feeling you get when you know something's not right but you can't quite put your finger on what it is.

Barely able to see the phone screen through my tears, I went to my call log and pressed my best friend Ajah's name. The phone rang twice before she picked up.

"Oh so, you finally remembered that I exist. I haven't heard from your triflin tail all day." She joked on the other end. "What do you want heffa?"

"Ajah…h-h-heee's gone!" I cried into the phone and then broke completely down. I was wailing into the phone like a child who'd just gotten an ass whooping.

"What? Who? Girl, you are scaring me! Who's gone? What happened?"

I could hear the panic in her voice, but I couldn't reply. I was crying too hard. My heart was shattered. I can't say if I was more hurt or afraid. I was afraid because I didn't know what I'd done to make him block me. At least if I had some idea of what was going on, I could fix it. Right now, in this moment, I had nothing. No way of contacting him. No idea as to where he was. Nothing. I thought about driving to his grandmother's house to see if he was there but quickly decided against it. I didn't want to be at his grandmother's house making a scene. If he'd blocked me that clearly meant he didn't want to talk to me. I felt hopeless.

"Yaya, you need to say something! You're scaring me." Ajah screamed on the other end and then I heard her mumbling. "Where the fuck is my gotdamn keys? I can't find shit when I need it." There was a brief pause. Then, I heard what sounded like keys jingling. "I'm on my way because I can't deal with you crying like this and not knowing what's going on."

"It's Choc." I managed to get out between sobs. "Ajah, he's g-g-gone."

"Gone where? Is he dead? Stop saying bits and pieces and talk!"

I pulled myself together the best I could. So that, I could respond. "I don't know where he is. He has me blocked on everything. I don't even know what I did. We were good when he left this morning."

"Giiiirl, I know you fuckin lying! Got me ready to drive clean across town at this time of the night because I'm thinking something bad done happened and you up here hootin and hollerin because this triflin motherfucka done disappeared again!" Ajah exploded. One thing about my bestie, she was gonna let me and anyone else know exactly how she felt, regardless to how it made them feel. She didn't have any filter at all. "Now you know, I'll ride for you anytime of the day or night but let's be realistic, Yaya. You know exactly what done happened. He laid up with some new slut bucket. Probably his dumb ass baby momma." I heard her suck her teeth. "Girl, if you don't hush that crying. He ain't g-g-gone. His sorry ass will be b-b-back, soon as he gets sick of her. You know his MO."

She was right, he had left before but the times before were different than this one. He'd never blocked me before. Just the thought of this brought on a whole new wave of fear. What if there was a new chick? What if she was the one? What if she made him happy in ways that I couldn't? What if he never came back? I broke down, again.

"Oh naw! Girl, if you don't pull yourself together and stop crying over him." Ajah's tone was a bit softer this time. "Yaya, I've told you time and time again. You can't change anyone, no matter how much you love them. They have to want to change. I know you love him, but don't you think you deserve that same type of love in return?"

I knew she meant well and the speech that she was giving was out of love, but I honestly didn't want to hear what she had to say. My mind was on one thing and one thing only. Finding Choc. "Ajah, I'm gonna call you back tomorrow." I sniffled, trying my best to stop crying. So, that I could gather my thoughts and try to figure out where Choc was and what was going on.

"Really? So, you're gonna get off the phone with me just to lay over there and cry and stress?" Ajah questioned.

I shook my head as if she could see me through the phone, while using the end of my night gown to wipe my snotty nose. "Nah, I'm I gonna clean myself up and go to

33

bed. My head hurts and I just want to lay down." Fresh tears spilled down my cheeks.

I heard Ajah let out a sigh. "Clean yourself up. I'm on my way."

"Nah, you don't have to come. I'm good." I objected. As much as, I didn't want to be alone. I didn't want to hear another speech, either. I just wanted to hurt in peace.

"Girl, I'm not about to allow you to be alone. I know, how hurt you are and regardless of how I feel you should or shouldn't handle things, I'm gonna be here for you." She explained. "Now, go dry those tears and I'll be over, shortly."

"Okay." I continued sniffling.

"Alright. See you soon."

****

Nearly an hour after getting off the phone with Ajah, my doorbell rang, followed by knocking. Knowing it was Ajah being silly at my door. I sucked my teeth as I rose from my bed to go answer the door. Now, dressed in a pair of oversized pajamas, a T-shirt, and fuzzy slippers. I dragged my feet as I made my way down the short hallway towards the door. When I reached the door, I swung it open and was a little shocked to see my sister, Mari, standing next to Ajah. Both in bonnets, sweats, and T-shirts and their hands filled with shopping bags. They'd come on a mission to cheer me up. This warmed my heart, knowing they'd dropped whatever they had going on to come and be by my side. Even if my pain at the moment was self inflicted. Regardless of the situation, I always knew I could count on them.

I shouldn't have been shocked at all seeing Mari with Ajah. I should've known that she would call Mari and inform her of what was going on because my sister and I had grown up with Ajah. She was more than our best friend, we were family. Our parents had grown up together and were the best of friends, as well. This thing with us went way back and ran deep. Our bond was definitely an unbreakable one.

"What are you doing here?" I asked, staring at my little sister.

"Standing outside like a stranger." Mari replied, stepping forward and embracing me as best she could with her hands full. "Now, move back and let me in."

I stepped back and she walked in, placing the bags down on the coffee table, before taking a seat on the sofa.

"I figured you could use the extra support." Ajah smiled, walking in.

I closed the door, walked over, and joined Mari on the sofa. Ajah went into the kitchen and returned with three wine glasses. Handing one to Mari and then one to me before placing one down on the coffee table. She reached in one of the shopping bags and retrieved a bottle of Merlot and poured some in each glass. Mari sat down her glass and began pulling more wine and snacks from the other shopping bags that they'd brought in.

Once everything was spread out on the coffee table, Mari picked up her glass, took a sip of wine, and asked. "So, what's our next move?"

"Damn, you make it sound like we're the mafia." Ajah giggled.

"Shit, we can be." Mari replied, with a shrug. "Because I can't lie. I for one am sick of this nigga's shit."

I took a large sip of my wine. I wanted to get tipsy as quickly as possible. In hopes that the alcohol would numb the pain I was feeling, and lessen the embarrassment I felt, as well. "I don't know what to do." I admitted, softly. I felt myself becoming emotional again and tried to suppress it but there was no use. The tears fell freely from my eyes, landing on my cheeks and shirt. "I know, I look stupid to y'all, sitting here crying over someone who obviously doesn't want me, but I can't help it. I do everything for this man..."

"And that's the problem!" Mari interjected. "You are doing everything for him, while accepting that he does nothing for you. His triflin ass can't even do the bare minimum. Respect doesn't cost a dime and he can't even give you that. Iyanna, I love you to death. So, I'm gonna keep it all the way real with you. Hopefully, this will help you pull yourself together..."

"Mari, don't tell her that." Ajah warned, cutting Mari off mid-sentence. She shook her head, looking over at me, she gave me a sympathetic look. "Not right now...I mean...not tonight."

"Girl, bye. If I tell her tomorrow, it won't be no better. She needs to know." Mari replied, before taking another sip of her wine, and then turning her attention to me. "Yaya, that nig…"

"Mari!" Ajah cut her off, again.

"What is it? Tell me." I wanted to know.

"Girl, he's back fuckin on his ex." Mari blurted. "After Ajah filled me in on what was going on and told me that he had blocked you. I went to his page. I saw where ol girl had tagged him in a picture on Facebook, announcing that they had finally gotten the keys to their new place. They were hugged up. She was holding the keys and he was standing next to her, looking like a piece of shit."

"Lordy, you are just messy." Ajah grabbed a bag of chips from the table and ripped them open. "Well, you may as well tell her the rest. Since, you told all of that." She suggested, shoving a few chips in her mouth.

"I ain't messy. Choc is the messy one!" Mari corrected.

I looked from Ajah to Mari, in disbelief of what I'd just been told. A part of me wanted to ask Mari to keep the rest of the information to herself but I knew I needed to hear it. "Just tell me!" I snapped.

"The ugly bitch is pregnant with another one of his baby seals. I swear, the other two he got with her look like sea creatures. I don't know why the fuck they keep laying down creating shit that looks like that." Mari delivered the final blow, while shaking her head, and wearing a disgusted expression. "I'm so glad you didn't allow that bastard to impregnate you."

It felt like the wind had been knocked out of me. Ajah and Mari were still talking but I couldn't hear a word because my mind was racing a mile a minute. So, much was going through my mind that I couldn't keep up. My body had been consumed by an overwhelming feeling of fear. This is why he'd been so nice to me, repeating how much he loved me and making me promise to love him no matter what. He'd been saying goodbye to me the night before and this morning. He'd chosen her, his baby momma. I'd lost him! He was moving in with Brie and they were having their third child. I could play dumb and act as if I didn't know what had just taken place, but the fact of the matter was, I'd always known the truth. I'd just prayed that my love for Choc would make him have a change of heart.

Brie was Choc's first love and on/off girlfriend. I'd met him during one of their off seasons. On the first date, he'd told me all about her. How much he loved her and how he'd tried to do everything to please her, but his best never seemed like enough. So, he'd decided to break things off and move on. I should've seen the big red flag, right then and there but my ignorant ass had ignored it. It was clear that he wasn't over this girl, but I got involved with him, anyways and tried my best to be everything that no other woman had been to him. However, it clearly didn't work. With all that I did, I still couldn't seem to get close to his heart. It was like he had a wall up and he only allowed me to get but so close. He told me he loved me and sometimes he showed it, but he was never consistent, and our relationship never progressed. We'd been at a standstill for the past year. I'd been trying to get him to move in for over a year, but he always said that he didn't want to move in with any woman. He'd been living with his grandmother since we'd met. At least, that's what he'd told me. He told me that when he moved out of his grandmother's house, he planned to get his own place. Said he wanted to finally live in a place that was all his with his name on the lease. I understood that. So, I didn't pressure him. I wanted him to have that independence. I figured that maybe if he got a place, I could just move in with him, but he'd obviously had a totally different plan in mind that didn't include my black ass. After wasting three years of my life, this black motherfucka was moving in with his fuckin ex.

My anger overtook me, and I hurled the wine glass in my hand across the room. Crashing against the wall, the glass shattered into pieces, sprinkling onto the floor like confetti. Next, I grabbed the open bottle of wine and threw that across the room. It hit the large plant, sitting over in the corner and then fell to the floor, spilling onto the carpet.

"I'm sick of this shit!" I screamed, furious. Tears streamed down my face, meeting beneath my chin. "I'm fuckin sick of being treated like a doormat! I've done everything for his black ass, and this is the thanks I get!" I fumed, rising to my feet. I kicked over the coffee table. All the snacks, wines, magazines, our phones, candles, and remotes tumbled onto the floor.

"Yaya, I know you're upset but this shit cost money!" Ajah shouted, reaching down and flipping the coffee table back into an upright position. She then began picking up the things that had fallen onto the floor.

Ignoring her, I continued! "Fuck them damn chips! Y'all think everything is a fuckin joke!" I accused, looking back and forth between Ajah and Mari. "This nigga did me dirty and you worried about some fuckin chips? What about how the fuck I feel?"

"You allowed the shit! This isn't the first time!" Ajah challenged, standing up right, closing the space between us, and getting in my face. "He's been doing you dirty and you've been taking him back! So yeah, I'm worried about the fuckin chips that I spent my damn hard-earned money on! Why am I gonna be worried about you, if you ain't worried about you? I love you to death, but I've come to realize that I have to let you do you until you get tired. I'm not about to keep wasting my breath and getting all worked up. Only for you to be laid right back up with that nigga when he comes back."

"You don't know what the fuck I'm gonna do!" I countered, getting so close in her space that our chests bumped.

"Alright y'all, that's enough!" Mari snapped, pushing her way in between us. She looked at Ajah. "Chill and allow her to have her moment. Regardless of whether or not she's gonna take him back. She deserves to have her moment to be pissed! Don't act like you ain't ever been there!"

"She can have all the moments she wants but not if it includes fuckin up my money." Ajah didn't back down.

"Bitch, I can give you that lil change you spent on that shit!" I snapped.

"Bitch, I would appreciate it! You are slanging my fuckin wine and chips across the room like you done lost your mind!"

"Would you bitches please shut the fuck up!" Mari screamed! Then placed her hand on her hip, looking at Ajah sideways. "And I bought the majority of that shit! Ajah, your cheap ass only gave me ten dollars."

That's all it took to change the entire mood. We all burst into laughter. That's how we were and it's also how you knew the love and bond we shared was real because one minute we could be ready to throw hands and the next we'd be laughing like nothing happened.

"I swear, y'all get on my damn nerves." Mari laughed, while stooping down to finish picking up the stuff from the floor. "We supposed to be mad at Choc and kickin his ass not each other's."

I looked at Ajah. "My bad for kicking over the stuff." I took a seat down on the floor, next to where Mari was now sitting.

Ajah took a seat, too. "My bad too for poppin off at you but you know black folks don't waste no food. Seeing, my chips hit that floor, touched a nerve."

"Girl, if you say one more word about them chips." Mari warned.

"What am I gonna do y'all?" I asked, becoming emotional, again.

"You gone stop all this crying and remember who the fuck you are and do what you need to do to move on." Ajah replied. "I know you love him but you've gotta stop allowing him to treat you like this. He's showing you how he feels about you. Believe him! He keeps running back to this girl, choosing her over you. Let her have lil dusty. Find you a nigga that puts you first and treats you like you should be treated. You're worthy of that. You do know that, right?"

"Yeah, I do." I sniffled, wiping my tears away.

"You're gonna be alright, girl. We got you." Mari assured leaning over and placing her arm around me.

Ajah moved closer and did the same. "Yeah, we got you."

For the next few hours, we sat on the floor talking, drinking, and snacking. Mari and Ajah left a little after 3:00 AM. Once, they were gone. I turned off all the lights in the front part of the house and staggered down the hallway to my bedroom. The wine that I'd consumed had me feeling nice. I kicked off my slippers and crawled into bed. After getting comfortable, I got on my phone and opened

Messenger. I saw that I had a message request. So, I clicked on it and saw that it was from Dro Turner.

Dro: *Just wanted to apologize again for getting out of character like that and disrespecting your home.*

Me: *I accept your apology.*

I replied with a smiley face emoji at the end. I closed Messenger and opened Facebook. After scrolling for a few minutes, my eyes began to get heavy. I closed the app, laid my phone down on the bed and turned over on my side. It wasn't long before I was fast asleep.

Dro

I felt bad about how I'd disrespected Yaya's house. I wasn't that type of nigga at all. Keema just had a way of getting under my skin like no one else could. My boys often teased me, saying that it was because I still had feelings for her but that couldn't be further from the truth. I had love for her because she was DJ's mother but nothing outside of that. Keema's selfish and hoeish ways had long diminished any feelings that I had for her. Being a mother hadn't changed her at all. Before, I could deal with her childish and petty ways because we were just two young motherfuckas looking for a good time, with only ourselves to think about but once DJ came along my entire mentality changed. I wanted everything for my son that I'd never had. So, I started moving differently. Don't get me wrong, I hadn't become some perfect dad that was flawless, but I was trying. Trying to be a better man. So, that I could raise my son to be a good man. I wasn't trying to raise a street nigga and have my son grow up and give the state years of his life or worst him end up dead due to some senseless bullshit. I knew there was always the possibility that he could still grow up and make those choices, but it wouldn't be because I didn't try to teach him better. That's why, I'd fallen back from the crowd. I still went out with the fellas every now and again but not like I used to. Now, I was working and focused on building a better life for me and my boy.

After putting DJ to bed, I looked up Yaya on Facebook. She wasn't hard to find because the salon she and Keema worked for had a Facebook page for business. I went to their business page and within seconds, I'd found her. I clicked on her name and sent her a message through Messenger apologizing. Once, I'd sent the message, I went back to her page. Something about the way she looked in the pictures on the salon business page was intriguing to me. I wanted to see more. As, I strolled down her page and through her pictures, I was thoroughly impressed by the things that I saw and surprised at the same time. I was expecting her to be wild and ratchet like Keema, but she wasn't. She seemed down to earth and well rounded. I learned by going down her timeline that she enjoyed reading, music, plants, and that she was a spiritual woman. I liked the fact that she was different. Different meaning, that she seemed open-minded. Looking through her pictures, I became mesmerized not just by how photogenic she was but by her style. Again, she did her own thing. She didn't appear to follow the trends. This woman was everything. I was shocked that no man had locked her down. Her relationship status was single and there were no photos of her with any men except her clients or family.

I stayed on her page for more than an hour. Before exiting, I sent her a friend request. I liked what I saw and wanted to see more.

After strolling Facebook for a while longer, I closed the app and checked my text messages. I had four from this chick named Juicy that I kicked it with from time to time. I hadn't kicked it with her in a few weeks though because she'd started getting too clingy and I'd made it clear to her that I wanted nothing more than sex with her. That was one thing about me, I didn't play games. I was straight up with anyone that I dealt with. Juicy was a really pretty girl. She had a cute round face, deep dimples, huge smile, full lips and these big brown eyes. She was a little on the chubby side, but I liked my women with meat on their bones. So, that was no problem for me. I also liked the fact that she had her own. She wasn't one of those chicks that was always complaining to a nigga about her bills or begging for help. She worked at the hospital as an RN, and she had a side hustle selling T-shirts. She was definitely a good woman, which was the thing that had attracted me to her. I didn't fuck with bums. There was nothing attractive about a lazy ass woman to me. It didn't matter how fine she was. If she wasn't about her business or at least trying to get her shit together. I wanted no parts of dealing with her. The same way women preached about knowing their worth, I knew mine, too and no bum bitches got a ride on this dick. However, with all the good qualities that Juicy possessed. I still wasn't interested in having a relationship with her. We didn't click in that way. The sex was great, though.

Juicy: *Hey. Wyd.*

Juicy: *Hellooo*

Juicy: *Are you asleep?*

Juicy: *I hope, I'm not coming off as crazy, but I miss you.*

All of her messages were within minutes of each other. She hadn't even given me time to read or respond to her first message. I had my read receipts on. So, she would've known if I'd read her messages. She was right. She was definitely coming off a little crazy. Even though, I didn't play games or beat around the bush. I wasn't a cold nigga and tried my best not to come off like an asshole or hurt anyone's feelings. Especially not someone as sweet as

Juicy but I knew I had to get some control over this situation before it got out of hand.

Me: *Hey. I'm chillin. I have my little man tonight. And nah, you're not coming off as crazy, but I feel that you may have the wrong impression about what this is or where it's going. I've made it clear from the beginning that I'm not looking to have a relationship. So, I wouldn't be leading you on in any way. With that being said. If you hit me up and I don't respond right away, there's no reason for you to message me back-to-back like I'm your nigga. I hope, I'm not coming off like an asshole but I'm just trying to keep shit 100 with you. That's why I haven't kicked it with you in a minute because you started to get too clingy. I think you're a dope female but you and I ain't like that. You feel where I'm coming from?*

After sending the text, I got up and went down the hall, and got in the shower. After the day that I'd had, this shower was pure love. It felt so good that I didn't want to get out, but I didn't want to be in the shower and DJ woke up looking for me and not see me. I didn't want him to be scared. So, I went ahead, washed up, and got out. When I was done, I slipped on a pair of boxers and then went into the kitchen and put a frozen pizza in the oven. I hadn't eaten anything since lunch that day and a nigga was on the brink of getting a headache. While my pizza was cooking, I went back into my bedroom to wait for it to get done. I turned on the tv and turned the volume down, since DJ was in my bed. The last thing I wanted to do was wake him and he be up the rest of the night. Sitting down on the side of the bed, I grabbed my phone and saw that Juicy had texted back.

Juicy: *Woooow. I mean, I know that you said you didn't want a relationship, but we been fuckin for like four months, now. I've even spent the night a few times and made breakfast the next morning in your kitchen. We lay up and talk and shit. You kissing all on me. That's definitely relationship vibes. It's like you told me one thing but carry shit different when I'm in your presence. So, I'm kinda confused but it's all good. I can fall back. I guess, you fuckin on a new bitch. That's really the issue. Fuck you, Dro! Clown ass nigga! I swear, you don't ever have to worry about me again!!!*

I looked at my phone in complete disbelief. This wasn't the sweet girl, Juicy, that I'd been kickin it with. The one who barely raised her voice or said a curse word. This bitch right here was trippin trippin! What the fuck was going on with all the females in my life tonight?

Me: *Clown ass nigga? I'm a clown because I'm being honest with you? So, you'd rather a nigga just play with your feelings and lead you on? Man, gtfoh! You the fuckin clown. Don't text my phone no fuckin more.*

This bitch had gotten me hot! I'd totally misjudged her. One thing was for sure though, she didn't have to worry about Dro, anymore. I'd promised myself after Keema that I wasn't dealing with anymore ratchet bitches and I meant that!

Juicy: *Fuck you and your phone! You always on Facebook preaching about being different from other niggas and talking about you can't find a good woman. You can't find a good woman because you ain't a good man! You don't know how to treat a good woman. You just want some convenient pussy and someone to suck your little ass dick.*

Juicy: *And I want the $20 for my fuckin shirt!*

She was really wildin. This crazy motherfucka had given me a shirt. I hadn't even asked for it. I decided not to respond and just block her. I didn't have time for this nonsense, and I wasn't about to give her another drop of energy. I knew that was what she wanted but she was about to be very disappointed.

I got up and went back into the kitchen. The smell of burnt crust smacked me in the nose the moment I entered the kitchen. "Shit! Tonight, just ain't my fuckin night!" I huffed, grabbing the dish towel. I opened the oven and saw that the top of the pizza looked edible, but the crust was very dark. "I'm finna eat the toppings off this motherfucka." I announced out loud. I walked over and got a paper plate off the counter. I used a spatula to plate the whole pizza on my plate. The crust was too hard to attempt cutting it. I went over to my utensil drawer and got a plastic fork. Then, walked over to the refrigerator and got a beer. I definitely needed some type of alcohol after the night I'd been having. I took everything back down the hall to my room. Placing my beer on the nightstand, I grabbed the folded bag of chips that had been lying on the nightstand for the past few nights and opened them up. I began eating my food and watching TV but my phone was going off every few seconds, alerting me that I had notifications. I hadn't posted anything on my social media. So, I had no idea as to why my phone was blowing up like this. I reached over and picked up my phone. On my home screen, I could see that everyone was commenting on a Facebook post that I'd been tagged in. What the fuck? I hurriedly unlocked my phone and went on Facebook. Only to see that

I'd been tagged in a post by Jayel SoJuicy Smith. I clicked on the post: *Dro Turner is a lying little dick clown ass nigga! Not only has this nigga been fuckin me and lying to me for the past 4 months but he owes me $20 dollars for a shirt! When I asked for my money he blocked me! All I want is my money! $20 may not be a big deal to y'all but I ain't got shit to give to a lying motherfucka for free! I got two kids to feed!* As if this post wasn't stupid enough, every female on it was going off, calling me every name but the child of God. They'd really taken this woman's side without knowing any of the facts. I wasn't one to put my business on Facebook, but this bitch wasn't about to lie on me, either. Knowing damn well, I hadn't lied to her or stole anything from her. I screenshotted the entire conversation that we'd just had and posted it in the comments along with a comment of my own…*Now, all you goofy ass, stale pussy bitches that was running y'all mouths can use your ashy ass lips to kiss my ass along with this delusion, thirsty, desperate ass bitch. Remember it's two sides to every story before you type your two cents next time or better yet, mind the business that pays y'all miserable asses.*

When I was done, I blocked Juicy on Facebook. I was done done with her ass. Mad as she had me at the moment, if I saw her ass crossing the street, I would stomp the gas and send that bitch straight to meet her maker.

With all that had transpired, I'd lost my appetite. I got up and took the rest of my picked over pizza into the kitchen and tossed it in the trash. When I got back to my room, I saw that the screen on my phone was glowing. I picked up my phone and saw that I had several messages from the group chat that I shared with a few of my homeboys. I also had a missed call from my cousin, Tre, who was more like a big brother to me. I knew that all the messages and the missed call were pertaining to the fiasco that had just taken place on Facebook. I was done giving energy to that situation for one night. So, I put my phone on Do Not Disturb and crawled into bed. I watched TV for a while before sleep consumed me.

****

The next morning, I woke up early and took DJ to the barbershop. After we were done there, we went to get breakfast at Cracker Barrel. While we were eating, Iyanna and two other females came in. I'd learned from her Facebook page that the brown skinned one was her sister, Mari and the lighter one was her best friend, Ajah. I was kind of surprised to see her in Roanoke, Rapids. Though, I'm not sure why because Boykins was literally right at the NC state line, and I was definitely glad that she'd chosen to cross that line this morning.

As the hostess lead Iyanna and her crew across the restaurant to their table, my eyes were glued to her. She'd come in wearing an orange sundress with the back out and her long dreads up in a high ponytail with an African print wrap around it. It was giving Janet Jackson in Poetic Justice vibes. I also noticed that her back was decorated in small tattoos. I couldn't make out what they were, but they definitely added to her sex appeal. The hostess seated them so that I had a clear view of their table. That made me feel a little uncomfortable because I didn't want to give off creep vibes if Iyanna happened to look up and catch me looking in her direction. I knew it would be impossible not to steal a glance or two. Since, she'd walked in looking like a fuckin goddess.

I made myself look away and refocused my attention on DJ, who was busy watching cartoons on his Ipad, with his thumb in his mouth and other hand playing with his ear. His food was in front of him, barely touched.

"DJ eat some of your eggs." I urged, while stirring the eggs, hoping that the ones on bottom were still kinda warm.

He glanced up at me and shook his head "no".

"Little boy, we ain't about to do this today." I spoke this time in a tone that let him know, I meant business. "You can either, eat or give me your iPad."

He shook his head "no" again, but this time, he reached over and grabbed a handful of eggs and stuffed them in his mouth.

I smiled, proudly. "That's daddy's big boy."

We finished our food, and I began cleaning DJ up so that we could leave. Out of nowhere, I heard a woman speaking to DJ. I looked up and saw Iyanna.

"Hey, DJ." Iyana spoke, standing next to his seat. "I thought that was you over here." Her eyes darted over to me. "Hey, Dro."

"Hey." I spoke, taking a better look at her now that she was close. Her eyes looked a little puffy and sad like she'd been crying but I figured maybe it was due to her not getting a lot of sleep. Puffy eyes and all, she was still a really attractive woman. I had to look away because I could feel myself becoming aroused.

"Hey." DJ replied, trying to get out of his seat.

"Hold on, boy. Let me help you down before you fall." I told him, while helping him out of his seat. Soon, as his feet touched the floor, he wrapped his arms around Iyanna's legs and then held up his arms for her to pick him up. She reached down and lifted him up in her arms.

He held out his hand. "Piece?"

"Oooo so that's why you wanted to get up here?" Iyanna laughed, sticking her hand down in her bag, retrieving a blow pop. She handed it to DJ, and he immediately started trying to unwrap it.

He shoved it back in her hand. "Open."

She looked over at me, with her mouth wide. "My bad, I didn't even ask you if he could have it. I'm so sorry. I'm just so used to giving him candy and Keema always lets him have it."

"It's fine." I assured her.

"You sure?"

"Yeah, go ahead. It's no problem." I watched as she unwrapped the blow pop and gave it to DJ. He took the candy from her and rested his head on her shoulder. He was very comfortable with her. I could tell that he was used to her and that she took time with him. This was the second time I'd seen my son with her. The first time was the night before and he'd been just as comfortable then as he was, now. This made me wonder how much time he was spending with her and just how close was she and Keema. Honestly, I hadn't really thought about her relationship with Keema too much the night before when I was on her page. She didn't have Keema tagged in a lot of posts on her page. The ones that Keema was tagged in were work related. It didn't look like they hung out but just because it wasn't posted on her social media didn't mean anything. There was no sense in me lying to myself. I was interested in getting to know Iyanna outside of Facebook, but I didn't want to approach her, and she turned me down because of her friendship with Keema. I knew for a fact that if the shoe were on the other foot, Keema wouldn't give a damn about Iyanna, but Keema was just selfish like that. Iyanna probably was the type that didn't believe in dating her friend's baby daddy and if that was how she felt, I could respect that. I wasn't worried about it causing any problems between her and Keema because Keema had fucked two of my homeboys and one of my cousins. She definitely had no reason to feel any kind of way about me trying to holla at Iyanna.

"Here you go." Iyanna said, interrupting my thoughts and bringing me back to the present. I held my arms out and she handed me, DJ. "My people are ready to go. So, I'm gonna get on up outta here and stop holding y'all up. I just wanted to run over here and speak to my little buddy." She waved at DJ. "Bye-bye, DJ."

"Bye-bye." DJ waved back at her.

"Alright then, Dro."

"Alright then, you take it easy."

"I'll try." She flashed me a smile and walked away in the direction of her friends, that were now standing a few feet away, waiting on her. They disappeared out the door and DJ and I headed out, as well.

<u>Choc</u>

"Babe, I'm so happy that we finally have our own spot." Brie smiled, placing my hand on her protruding belly. "We finally got our shit together and is on the same page but most importantly we're giving our children the family they deserve."

"Yeah." I replied, not really interested in the conversation. My mind was somewhere else. I felt bad about how I'd done Yaya. She didn't deserve the fucked-up way that I'd left her with no explanation. It'd been two weeks now since I'd last spoken to her. I knew she was hurt by my actions, but I had no choice. There were things Yaya didn't know about my situation with Brie. From the outside looking in and not knowing the full story, it would appear that I was just running back and forth between the two because I could. That was partially true but there was a bigger issue at hand. Brie's mental health wasn't good at all. She'd been battling depression since her teens. As a result, she'd dabbled in drugs over the years. Cocaine and percs being her drugs of choice. Her addiction had nearly claimed her life twice. The most recent time being a few months ago. Luckily, she hadn't lost the baby, but the doctor had warned that the baby could be born with abnormalities due to Brie's overdose. After that scare, her mom had made her go to rehab with threats of taking the kids, if both of us didn't get our shit together. She'd given us ninety days to find a place of our own or she was going to family court and file for custody of the kids. She'd even threatened to take the new baby once it was born. Of course, I couldn't allow her to take the kids. Even though, I knew she would take good care of them, and they would probably be better off. I felt I owed it to them to get my shit together and do my best to keep them with us. If they grew up and learned that we let them be raised by their grandparents because we couldn't get our shit together and do right by them. I knew they'd never forgive us and rightfully so. As a man and as a father, I knew I needed to step up to the plate and do what needed to be done by any means necessary.

I can't lie, there were times that I'd thought about leaving Brie, taking my kids, and settling down with Yaya. I knew, without a doubt, Yaya would be good to my kids and treat them like her own, but I couldn't do Brie like that. She was their mother. She had her issues, but I didn't feel she deserved that. She deserved for me to try harder to help her. I owed that to her. At times though, helping her seemed damn near impossible. I loved her but her issues were a lot to deal with. When she was good, things were great but when she slipped back into one of her bouts with depression. Shit was crazy. On top of that, she was super insecure and overly jealous. I don't know if that was a part of her depression or what but sometimes, I felt like I was drowning in her issues, and I just needed some type of peace. That's where Yaya came in. Yaya provided me with a sense of peace, an escape from all the madness. When I was with Brie, everything was all about her and all of her issues. With Yaya, I got a chance to express myself and the things that I wanted without seeming selfish. She actually asked me about me, my feelings, my goals and my dreams. I couldn't express those things to Brie and of course, she never asked or seemed interested in knowing anything about what I had going on. There was no room for me in our relationship. Just her and her needs. That was one of the things that led to my cheating. I'm not saying it made it right, but I needed things in a relationship that I couldn't get from Brie. My cheating was about more than sex.

Don't get it twisted, Brie was no saint when it came to the infidelity in our relationship. She'd cheated on me as well. Of course, she'd blamed it on the drugs. Saying she wasn't in her right mind when she'd cheated but I didn't give a damn about that. High or sober, she'd still cheated. I guess, there were things that she needed that I couldn't provide, either because I wasn't about to support her drug habit in no way, shape, or form. Honestly, if it wasn't for the love I held in my heart for her, I would've left her ass as soon as I found out that she was getting high, but I couldn't just turn my back on her. Especially not with my kids being in her care. So, I felt obligated to try and help her beat her addiction and get better. I tried my hardest to provide all that she needed when it came to being supportive and loving her but still, she would always end up relapsing. I'd become convinced that when it came to Brie, there wasn't a man or woman walking the earth that was capable of providing what she needed. She needed a partner, caregiver, and therapist all rolled into one. I'd left multiple times because of how overwhelming our situation was. Shit, she'd left me, too. But somehow, we always ended up right back together, though. Whether it was because of me feeling guilty for leaving because of her condition or whether it was because of the kids or simply because we actually missed each other. We always ended up right back where we'd left off.

During one of our breakups, I'd met Yaya. The day I met her, I was at the Chinese spot ordering some food and she'd come in. I'd finished placing my order and was now waiting for my food. I took a seat at one of the vacant tables, checking her out as she ordered. I had never seen her around before and if I had, I couldn't remember. Which makes absolutely no sense because I doubt if I would've forgotten her face. She would've stood out, I'm sure. Just like, now. Her beauty demanded my attention. Her light brown eyes were hypnotizing, a perfect complement to her smooth chocolate complexion. Her lips were full and pouty, giving off a seductive look. Her hair was loc'd. She had it pulled back into a ponytail, showing off a fresh face with no makeup. Allowing me to see every inch of her natural beauty. My eyes roamed from the wooden pair of African-inspired earrings that dangled from her ears, down to the all black ensemble that she wore. A long pea coat, thick leggings, Uggs, and a thick fuzzy scarf. She was definitely dressed to combat the icy January weather but even with her body hidden away beneath all those layers of clothing, I could tell that she was beautiful all over and different from the females that I'd dealt with. Her style was confident and classy. This woman was pressure, effortlessly. I was instantly mesmerized and couldn't tear my eyes away from her.

When she was done ordering her food, she took a seat at one of the other empty tables and took out her phone. I wanted to say something to her, but I wasn't sure of what to say. She looked like the sophisticated type, and I didn't want to say anything stupid and end up coming off childish. She kept her head in her phone until the door opened and an older white gentleman entered, letting in a gust of cold air. She looked at the door with wrinkles decorating her beautiful face.

"Damn, it's cold." She complained, placing her phone down on the table and pulling her scarf up around neck a little tighter. Then, she cupped her hands around her mouth and blew her warm breath into them, before rubbing them together.

That was my opening. "Hell yeah. It is cold as shit." I agreed. "That's why I got me a large container of chicken and rice soup."

"Mmmmm...that sounds good, but I don't eat chicken." She replied and then added. "I should've gotten some egg drop or vegetable soup, though." Without another word, she sprang to her feet and went back to the register.

"Excuse me." She spoke to the middle-aged woman at the register.

"Yeah, how may I help you?" The woman asked.

"Can I add a large vegetable soup to my order?"

"Yes, ma'am. Will that be all?"

"Yes, ma'am."

"It will be ready in ten minutes."

"Okay."

"Thanks." She told me as she sat back down.

"No thanks needed." I smiled. "Glad I could help."

She smiled and looked back down at her phone. I didn't want to let her leave without at least trying my hand at getting her number.

"Excuse me." I called to her.

She raised her head and looked at me. "Me?"

"Yeah…ummm…are you from out this way? I can't remember ever seeing you."

"I'm sure you see lots of people on a daily basis. So, it would be next to impossible to remember seeing me." She laughed, showing off the sexy gap between her two front teeth. I'd always found gaps to be sexy. This just made her even more attractive.

"I would've definitely remembered if I'd seen you before."

"Yeah…ok."

"I'm serious." I laughed and then asked, again. "So, are you from this area or you just passing through?"

"I'm from Boykins."

"Oh okay. I come to Boykins quite often. My grandma Lizzie lives out there. I'm originally from Murfreesboro, NC, though. That's where my mom and most of her family live. I was living here in Franklin, but I've been back in Murfreesboro for about two months, now. I moved back there to stay with my grandma, Doris. She's been having some health issues."

"Sorry to hear that. I hope she gets well soon."

"Thanks. I appreciate that."

"No problem." She smiled and then added. "I know a few people from Murfreesboro. A few of my regular clients are from Murfreesboro."

"Clients?"

"Yes. I do hair. I'm a loctician. I specialize in locs but I can do damn near anything a client wants done." She smiled, proudly.

"Okay…okay." I nodded, impressed. "You work at a shop or do hair at your house?"

"Both actually but I work at a salon by the name of Posh. I'm not sure if you've heard of that…"

"Yeah…I have." I interrupted. "Boykins ain't but so big. So, if you've been to Boykins, you pretty much know all the spots."

"Okay, my bad and don't be trying to come for my hometown. Talking about Boykins ain't but so big." She laughed, rolling her eyes playfully. That showed me, she had a sense of humor. I liked that.

"My bad. I didn't mean any harm." I held my hands up in surrender.

"Mmmhmmmm. Well anyways, I've worked at Posh for the past ten years."

"Ten years?" I questioned, wondering if she was pulling my leg because she didn't look old enough to have worked anywhere for the past ten years.

"Yes."

"Wait a minute. How old are you if you don't mind me asking?"

"I'm thirty-four." She smiled, proudly.

"Hell naw!" I shook my head, thinking that she was lying because she looked like she couldn't have been more than twenty-five. "You're lying your ass off."

"I'm dead serious. I was born in 1985."

"Sir, your order is ready." The Korean woman behind the register called, interrupting our conversation.

"Hold on. We ain't done." I told the beautiful liar sitting in front of me. As I got up and walked towards the counter to grab my food.

"Ma'am your order is ready." The woman behind the register looked past me at Yaya.

"Oooh good." Yaya replied, getting up from her seat and shuffling to the counter behind me.

After getting my food, I walked outside and waited for Yaya to come out. Something about her made me want to do whatever it took to get next to her. I wasn't even the type of nigga to be doing the most for no female because I had bitches willing to do the most to get next to me. There was something different about Yaya, though. There was something about her energy that had me intrigued and made me want to be in her presence no matter what it took.

A big smile spread across her lips when she emerged from the restaurant and saw me leaning against the building, waiting for her.

"So, this the type of time you on?" She blushed, never stopping.

"Hell, yeah." I admitted, proudly, falling into step next to her. "Now, for real. How old are you?"

"I'm thirty-four." She told me, hitting the unlock button on her keychain, pointed at a black Honda Accord.

"Damn. I don't know what you're doing but keep doing it because you are aging backwards." I complimented her, still not fully believing that she was telling me the truth.

"Thanks." She smiled, opening the back door of her car and placing her food inside then closing the door. She looked at me as she opened the driver's door. "Well, it was nice talking to you..."

"Justin but everyone calls me Choc. I don't like Justin. Sounds like a white boy's name."

Her eyes rolled up in her head as she smacked her lips. "Boy, please. Your name doesn't sound like a white boy's name. The name Justin isn't exclusive to only white people. Why do black people think like that? I hate it."

"Whoa...chill. It ain't that deep. I was half joking, but I honestly don't know a lot of black Justin's. Calm down." That had gone completely left.

She let out a small chuckle and I was relieved to see the smile return to her lips. "I apologize for snapping. I just don't like it when people say stuff like that. I think it's ignorant and close minded. Like black people can only have ghetto ratchet names or should I say unique names."

Hoping to shift the mood back, I asked. "Well, what's your name?"

"Iyanna but everyone calls me Yaya."

"Yaya…I like that."

"Well, that's nice to know. It's not too white for you." She laughed.

"I see you're not gonna let that go, huh?"

"Yeah, I was just being silly."

"Well, it's chilly out here. So, I don't want to keep holding you up, but I would love to get to know you better. So, can I get your number?"

She looked at me for a few seconds, like she was contemplating. Then, she replied. "Yeah. I guess, you can have my number."

"You guess?" I laughed, taking out my cell and going to my contacts. "Okay. I'm ready." She then proceeded to call out her digits. When I was done saving her in my contacts. I told her that I would give her a call later. We said goodbye and went our separate ways.

Over the next few weeks, we talked every day and went out every weekend. Yaya was the complete opposite of Brie. Her conversation was more mature. We talked about everything, and she wasn't selfish. She was very kind, thoughtful, and attentive. She asked about my dreams and aspirations. She encouraged me to go after what I wanted and to be fearless, whether things worked out or not. She was so confident that I felt intimidated. She was so comfortable in her skin and focused. She knew exactly what she wanted. She was also a straight shooter. She didn't bite her tongue at all. I liked how she seemed to have it all together but at the same time, that made me feel like I wasn't good enough. Not because of anything that she said or did to make me feel that way but because of my own insecurities. For years, I'd been talked down to by my family and Brie. So, that shit had become programmed in my head. Even with having a woman, who now spoke life into me. I still kept hearing all the negativity that had been told to me over the years, in the back of my mind. I wanted to be as great of a man as Yaya believed I could be, but my fears stood in my way.

Things were good between Yaya and me. I really liked her a lot and had developed strong feelings for her, but those feelings hadn't been strong enough to keep me from going back to Brie. As much as I enjoyed being with Yaya, whenever I was around Brie, I felt guilty about being so happy when she was still fighting mental demons and not able to go on with her life and be truly happy. A part of me felt like I knew that Brie would be mentally able to care for herself and the kids. I could probably move on with Yaya and be happy. Seeing Brie so mentally broken and lost, tugged at my heart. I couldn't be happy knowing that she wasn't. So, I went back to her because I felt that she needed me and of course because I still loved her. However, this time was different because Yaya was now in the picture. So, I was constantly trying to divide my time between the two of them and keep them both happy. Which eventually caught up with my ass. Brie had become suspicious that I was dealing with someone else but every time she asked, I denied her accusations. So, one night while I was asleep. She went through my phone and found pictures and messages, confirming my relationship with Yaya. She called Yaya and told her who she was and that she and I were still very much together. Then, she woke me up and informed me that she'd spoken to my 'bitch'. Of course, they were both pissed at my ass but honestly, I had no fear of losing Brie because I knew that I could eventually smooth things over with her. On the other hand, I'd been terrified that Yaya might never fuck with me again. After getting curse out by Brie, I'd left and gone straight to Yaya, pleading my case and apologizing. Fortunately for me, by now, Yaya had fallen in love with me. This worked in my favor because even though, I'd hurt her. She wasn't ready to throw in the towel and give up on us. So, she forgave me and took me back. Of course, I promised her that I was done with Brie but that was a lie. I continued to lie to them both and it worked for a while until Brie's latest episode. I'd even been able to keep Brie's pregnancy a secret but just like before all of my lies had eventually caught up with me. Now, here I was back with Brie, unhappy, and feeling trapped.

"Choc, did you hear anything, I just said?" Brie's voice and her nudging my arm interrupted my thoughts.

"Yeah...I heard you." I lied.

Twisting her full, pink lips up and rolling her eyes. She asked. "What did I just ask you, then?"

I let out a frustrated breath because I knew that she was about to get on my nerves. I wasn't in the mood for her shit. I honestly wished that she'd go into another room and give me some space. She'd been stuck to my ass like glue since we'd moved in. I couldn't make a move without her. "I'd zoned out. I was thinking about something. What did you say?"

"Don't even worry about it!" She snapped, getting up and moving to the sofa, leaving me on the loveseat. "You've been acting funny since yesterday! Probably over there thinking about one of your bitches! Probably, that bitch, Yaya. What is it about her that you can't seem to let go and just focus on me and your kids?"

"Brie don't start." I told her. I didn't feel like discussing Yaya with her, but I knew without a doubt that she wasn't going to let it go. It was as if she was obsessed with Yaya or something.

"Nah, I want to know." Brie continued. "Yeah, you're here with me, trying to do the right thing but I can tell you miss her. You've been moping around here for the past two weeks like a sad puppy. You act as if you've lost your best friend."

"Brie, let it go. I'm good. I ain't even thinking about that girl. I'm here with you and my kids. That's all that should matter. Why are you trying to start an argument?"

"I'm not. I just don't want you here out of pity. Don't get me wrong. I'm glad that you are trying to do the right thing but who wants to be with someone, who is only with them because they feel obligated to be?" She paused, shaking her head. "I know everyone is afraid that if you leave, I will go on another binge or try to hurt myself but honestly, you being here won't stop that. Only I can stop that. You being here helps but you can't monitor me 24/7. That's impossible. If I want to do drugs, I eventually will. What you and my family don't understand is, I was unhappy long before you. When I met you, you became my distraction from the pain for a while, but distractions are only temporary. That hurt doesn't completely go away. It's still there and until I get the help, I truly need. It will never go away. Nobody can save me but me."

I got up, walked over and sat next to her on the sofa. "Well, if you know that. Then, why won't you get the help that you need because until you do this will be a losing battle for us, no matter what I do."

"I've tried getting help. I've talked to several therapists and did rehab programs. It all just seems to be a temporary fix. Eventually, I become depressed again and then, I start craving the drugs to escape the pain." She dropped her head. "I don't know, if there is anything that can help me to overcome all of the confusing feelings that I feel. I honestly feel helpless."

I saw tears rolling down her cheeks and felt sorry for her. It had to be hard living with the feeling of being helpless. I reached over and pulled her into my arms. "Don't cry. You aren't helpless. We just have to find you the right doctor, who can help you but Brie, you have to try. You have to fight this depression for the kids and for me. I'm trying baby but I can't make this work by myself."

"I know, you probably love Yaya because she isn't all fucked up like me." She sobbed into my chest. "How can I compete with that?"

Damn, she had me feeling like shit because she was partially right. I did love the fact that Yaya was easier to deal with and things with her were so much easier but that wasn't my sole reason for loving her. "Baby, you don't have to compete with anyone. Yaya isn't even an issue anymore. I'm here with you, focusing on us. I just need you to stop thinking about the past and focus on what's going on right now. Focus on getting better. So that we can raise our kids and be the best parents that we can be for them."

"I'm trying but it's hard. I keep thinking of the harm that I've possibly already caused this baby growing inside of me and I can't lie. Every time I think about our baby being born with defects due to my drug use, I want to get high. I don't want to feel the guilt of what I may have done to my unborn child. I just want to escape this feeling."

"You can't do that. You can't give in to that feeling. You have to be strong and fight it. Keep in mind what your mom said. I know, you don't want her to take our kids and raise them as her own. If she gets them, she may not allow you to see them. I know for a fact that you don't want that."

Even though, I didn't believe her mom wouldn't allow her to see the kids if she took them. I had to tell her that.

Brie shook her head, using her hand to wipe away her tears. "I don't but I don't know how to fix me. It's just so hard. Nobody understands how I feel."

"I don't but I'm trying. I'm here for you in any way that I can be. Just tell me what you need."

"I DON'T KNOW!" She yelled, visibly frustrated.

"Research somethings you can do to help to help cope with your depression. Look up some doctors. Stop saying what you can't do and try. It only wins when you give up."

"When did you become a motivational speaker?" Brie wanted to know.

"I'm not. I just be trying to look at shit in more than one way. Instead of only looking at the negative in a situation. I try to figure out a positive solution."

"Wow, where did this new positive Choc come from? I mean, I like it but I'm just a little surprised that's all."

I shrugged my shoulders. "I've told you. I'm trying to change and be better. That's all."

"Mmmmhmmm." Brie eyed me suspiciously. "I hear you. Well, I'm proud of you and I appreciate you being here and trying to do what's right for me and the kids. I apologize for making things more difficult. I don't mean to be this way. I'm going to try harder to get better and meet you halfway."

I leaned over and pressed my lips against her forehead. "That's all I want is for you to try."

She tilted her head upward and puckered her lips. I accepted the invitation and covered her lips with mine. She was the first to pull back. "I'm going to try and stop throwing Yaya in your face, too. If we're going to move forward and try to make this work. I know, I need to stop bringing her up. So, from now on, I'm leaving her in the past along with the drugs and negative thoughts."

A smile spread across my lips. "Now that's what I'm talking about!" I pulled her into a hug while kissing the top of her head. "We got this, babe."

"Yeah, we got this!" She echoed.

"Ma, can we have some chips?" Justice, our oldest, asked as he entered the room. Jada our youngest followed, stopping next to him with her thumb in her mouth.

Brie sat up, wiping her face, trying to pull herself together. "I'll get y'all some in a minute, Justice. Go back to your room."

"I can get them." Justice offered.

"You can't get them. You ain't tall enough."

"I'll do it. You just sit here and chill out for a little while." I told Brie while getting up from the sofa and scooping Jada up in my arms. "Come on in the kitchen, Justice."

"Can we have juice, too?" Justice wanted to know.

"Yeah, y'all can have juice, too." I chuckled. He loved to eat. "When y'all finish your snack. I'll take y'all to the playground for a little while. So, your mama can relax and have a little peace and quiet. How about that?"

"Yay!" Justice cheered.

"You wanna go to the playground?" I asked Jada while placing her in one of the chairs at the table.

She nodded her head, still sucking on her thumb.

I grabbed two snack sized bags of Cheetos from the cabinet and then got two juice boxes out of the fridge. After giving both kids their snacks, I took a seat at the table to wait for them to finish and to ensure that Jada didn't make a mess.

I sat at the table, replaying the conversation between Brie and I over in my head. I hoped that Brie actually meant everything that she'd said about trying to do better and get better. That was the only way that shit was going to work out between us. She had to do her part. I was going to allow her time to put some action behind her words but if I didn't see her actually trying soon. I would be forced to step in and start doing some research of my own. I hadn't gone through with getting a place with her and hurting Yaya, all for nothing. This shit had to work. I didn't want to end up resenting Brie because I'd chosen her, and she'd refused to do her part. Every moment, since I'd walked out of Yaya's door, I'd questioned if I'd made the right decision. I knew exactly what I had in Yaya. She was a good woman, willing to do anything for me. She not only told me how she felt about me, but she showed it in the things that she did for me and the way that she spoke to me. She showed it in the way that she was patient with me. It had taken a lot for me to walk away from her and risk losing her to someone else. The worst part of it all was, I knew that she was thinking the worst of me right now. Thinking I'd just walked out on her and not given a fuck about her feelings. That couldn't be further from the truth. I hated how I'd left things with her. I wished that I'd been less of a coward and explained to her what was going on and why I needed to end things with her, but I honestly hadn't wanted to see her cry. I just couldn't stand to see the hurt on her face.

Letting out a frustrated breath, I rubbed my head and then glanced over at Jada. She was rubbing Cheetos in her hair.

"Lord have mercy, girl." I said, taking the Cheetos from her, which caused her to start crying and throwing a fit. "No ma'am. You are not about to start that falling out mess." I told her.

She continued to kick and cry, and then slapped the bag of Cheetos on the floor. She'd been displaying this new little attitude for the past few weeks. Brie found it cute. Talking about it was a little toddler tantrum. I didn't find it cute at all and I wasn't about to tolerate it. If she was slapping shit across the floor every time, she got mad, now. At three years old. I could only imagine what she would be doing if I allowed this to continue.

Smacking her on her legs twice. I told her to get up, pick the bag of chips up, and put them in the trash. She got down from the chair and did as she was told. Crying as if I had nearly killed her. "Girl, hush that noise before I give you something to cry for."

She walked back over and rested her head on my leg, still sniffling. I picked her up and sat her on my lap. She laid her head on my chest and put her thumb in her mouth. That told me, she was sleepy. So, I rocked her back and forth.

"Are we still going to the playground?" Justice inquired, chewing a mouthful of Cheetos.

"Yeah, let me get your sister to sleep, first. Then, me and you will go to the playground."

"Can I take my ball?"

"Yeah, you can take your ball."

I sat rocking Jada until I heard her snoring, softly. Once, I knew that she was really out, I got up and took her down the hall to the room that she shared with Justice and laid her down on the air mattress. After, wrapping her up. I told Justice to put on his shoes. When he was done. He grabbed his ball, and we headed down the hall. As we were passing through the living room, I stopped and let Brie know that Jada was asleep and that I was taking Justice to the playground for a little while.

"How you figure, I didn't want to get out of the house and get some fresh air?" She wanted to know.

"We can't all go out and leave Jada back there asleep. I figured you could chill, and I take him out. That way, you will be kids free for a little while." I replied, hoping that she wasn't about to start her bullshit. "Do you want to take him to the playground while I stay her with Jada?"

She wrinkled up her face, waving me off. "Nah, go ahead. I'm just tired of being cooped up in the house. I want to go out and do something." She complained, while picking up the remote and turning on the TV.

Letting out a sigh, I rubbed my head, trying not to snap. "Brie, you know I used most of the money I had saved up to get this apartment and to get all of the utilities turned on. Plus, we needed furniture and stuff. So, we really ain't got it like that to be going out. I have a little money put up but I'm trying to use that wisely, not knowing what might come up. If we have some type of emergency, I want to be able to take care of it and not be out here begging and bumming from your parents or any of my family."

Brie threw up her hands, being super animated and dramatic. "Lord have mercy! Do you have to go into a whole speech about everything. Don't get me wrong. I'm glad you've changed and is trying to be all responsible and whatnot but damn. I wasn't asking for a trip to Disneyland. I was referring to something a little cheaper like maybe going out for dinner or maybe to the movies or we could go over to Ms. Lizzie's and play cards or something. We can afford to do something without spending your entire little emergency fund."

"See? That's the shit that be pissing me off. The way that you come out of your mouth, talking about *your little emergency fund*. You had made your point. You didn't even have to say that last little part. You should be happy a nigga is even thinking like that because a few years ago. I wouldn't have been thinking ahead or trying to prepare for shit."

"I'm glad that you're thinking ahead, I just don't want to hear a whole fuckin speech every time I ask you a simple question." She exploded, sucking her teeth. "I guess, this is just how niggas start acting once they done had a taste of a bougie bitch." She shook her head.

And just that quickly, she was back to throwing Yaya in my face. "Man, I'm out. I don't have time for this stupid shit." I walked over and snatched the front door open. "Come on, Justice." He ran out into the hallway.

"I forgot. I'm not supposed to bring up your bitch! My bad!" Brie called after me, tauntingly.

I didn't respond to her. I simply closed the door in her face.

When Justice and I arrived at the playground, there were a few other kids there. So, he went over and started to play with them. I took a seat on one of the benches and took out my phone. I opened Facebook and strolled for a while. Wasn't much going on up there. So, I closed it and went to my block list on my phone. I stared at Yaya's name for a minute, contemplating whether I should unblock her and call. I can't lie, I missed her but that wasn't the reason I wanted to call. I really wanted to apologize. Knowing how badly I'd hurt her had me feeling guilty as hell. I really did love her a lot. I stared at Yaya's number for a few more moments before doing what I'd really been wanting to do. I unblocked her and pressed the phone icon. Putting the phone up to my ear, I listened to it ring, wondering if she'd even answer.

"Oh so, you decided to unblock me?" Yaya answered.

"Yeah…I'm sorry about that." I began but she cut me off.

"Save your sorry for someone, who wants to hear it because I don't. You made a choice. So, stand on that. Don't get on my line lying. What do you want, Choc?" She was straight to the point.

"Yaya, I didn't call to argue…"

She cut me off, again. "Ain't nobody arguing." She let me know and then repeated. "What do you want?"

I let out a sigh. I should've known this shit wouldn't be simple as I'd wanted it to be. "I called to apologize for the way I left shit. It wasn't right and I feel fucked up about it. You're a good woman. You didn't deserve that. I should've been man enough to tell you what the deal was, but I couldn't. I didn't know how. I didn't want to hurt you."

She began laughing. "You didn't want to hurt me. Is that some kind of joke or something?"

"Nah, man. I know, I still hurt you and I'm sorry for that. The shit was fucked up. I know that."

"Oh, you do?"

"Yaya come on, man. Don't make this shit harder than it already is. I know, you don't believe me when I say I'm sorry for hurting you but I really am. I love you."

"Nah, that's bullshit. You don't love me because you don't hurt someone you love. You love your baby mama, not me."

"I love you both." I blurted. That shit kinda just slipped out but fuck it. It was the truth. "It may sound fucked up, but I do. I love you both for different reasons. She has my kids though, Yaya. And there's things about our situation that you don't know. Shit, you may or may not understand. I probably...naw...I should've explained

88

things to you. Instead of just walking out with no explanation but at the time. I honestly didn't believe it would make a difference. I knew that no matter how I explained it. You would still be hurt. So, I took the coward way out and just left."

"Okay. So, why are you on my line? I was minding my business. Why are you bothering me? Do you think that a fuckin apology changes anything? Do you think any of this shit you're saying makes me hurt any less? Three…fuckin years, Choc. Three years of my life, I've given you." Her voice began to crack. She was crying. That made me feel like shit. "I loved you through all the bullshit you put me through because I honestly believed that in the end you would choose me." She let out a chuckle and I heard her sniffling. "I thought, you would choose me because you would see how much I love you, but that shit didn't mean a thing. You got out of my bed that morning and left as if nothing was wrong and then, I find out that I've been blocked and that you had moved in with your baby mama. Not only did you move in with her but y'all have another baby on the way. Another baby that was made while you were laying up with me, telling me, you love me! Then, you have the nerve to call me with some weak ass apology, talking about you love us both? The love you have for me, you can give it to her because I don't want or need it! Fuck you! Fuck them kids! And fuck your goofy ass baby mama! Y'all can all kiss my ass! Oh yeah and fuck your weak ass apology!" With that, she hung up.

I took the phone from my ear, shoved it back in my pocket and took out my cigarettes. Shaking one from the pack, I placed it between my lips and fished my lighter from my pocket. Lighting my cigarette, I took a long drag before removing it from my lips and holding it between my fingers. I glanced over at Justice to make sure that he was good. He looked like he was having the time of his life. I envied him. I wished that I could go back to his age when life was simple, with no responsibilities. However, wishing wasn't going to change anything. I'd gotten myself in a fucked-up situation.

My thoughts went back to Yaya. I'd never in the three years that I'd been dealing with her, heard her snap like that. I understood it, though. That was her pain talking. Everything she'd just said was true except that I didn't love her. I did and it didn't matter whether she believed me or not because I knew that I did. If I didn't, I wouldn't care about how she felt but I did. This love shit was just crazy.

As I sat there, looking out across the park and smoking my cigarette. My grandma Lizzie's favorite

warning popped in my head, *If you make your bed hard,*
remember you've gotta lay in it. She was damn sure right
about that. I'd chosen Brie over Yaya, and I wasn't sure if
I'd chosen correctly but whether the choice was right or
wrong. I had to live with it, now.

****

After taking Justice back home. I decided to ride
over to my grandma Lizzie's shot house. I asked Brie if she
wanted to go but she declined. She was still upset from
earlier. So, I just let her be because I was tired of talking
and tired of arguing. I was just plain fuckin tired at this
point. Maybe, it was best that she stayed home, and I went
alone to give each other some space. We'd been up under
each other a lot the past two weeks except for when I was
at work. We could use a break from each other, and I could
definitely use a few moments of peace.

I pulled up to Grandma Lizzie's place a little after five that evening. There were a few cars in the yard, which wasn't surprising. There was always someone there. Especially the old heads. They woke up ready to drink. Some of them just came to sit around and talk. They were probably there to escape whatever they had going on at home, like me.

I parked my car, got out, and went inside. The door was rarely locked. I hated that. I'd said something to grandma about this numerous times, but it was obvious that she didn't listen.

"Who in the hell is that walking up in my house without knocking?" I heard grandma calling from the den.

"If your door was locked, no one could walk in." I shouted, walking into the den.

Grandma was seated in her favorite chair with two bags of white potatoes at her feet, a bowl in her lap with freshly peeled potatoes, and a dollar general bag next to her that held peelings from the potatoes she had already peeled. I knew that meant she was about to start selling plates. She always sold dinner plates to her night customers. She was one of the hardest hustling women, I knew. She was always gonna get a dollar. Age hadn't slowed her down one bit. Reaching down, she grabbed another potato and began peeling it. Glancing up at me, she said. "That's a good way to get a few caps put in your ass."

"Grandma, you ain't gone shoot nobody." I laughed, walking over and kissing her on her cheek. Then, I went over and took a seat in one of the wooden chairs at the table.

"Alright, keep thinking that." She warned. The dark brown juice from the snuff in her bottom lip, painted the corners of her mouth. She'd dipped snuff for as long as I could remember, and I hated it. I always found it to be disgusting but I knew it was something she would never give up. The most disgusting part was the spit jar, she kept with her to spit out the juice. When me and my cousins were younger, she would make us empty it and wash it out. I despised that shit. I was so glad when I got old enough to tell her no when she asked me to touch it. I would do anything for my grandma because I knew she would do anything for me but touching that nasty ass jar was where I drew the line.

"Your tail gonna end up in jail and I ain't gonna bail you out." I teased, knowing I would sell everything I owned to get her out at the drop of a dime.

"That's fine. I don't need you to bail me out. I'm woman enough to do the time if I do the crime." She let me know.

"You're one sassy little woman." I laughed and she did too.

"Now, what is your narrow tail doing over here? You must want something because you don't come around here unless you do."

"I just came through to holla at my granny. Is that a crime?"

She shook her head, never bothering to look up from what she was doing. "Nah, it ain't but I know you. So, I know it's something."

"I don't mean to interrupt y'all, but can I get another shot of gin, Lizzie?" One of her regulars, Mr. Herman, asked.

"Choc, go in there and pour Herman a shot of gin." Grandma told me. "And don't get happy handed with my bottle either. There's a shot cup in there to measure."

"Grandma this ain't my first time serving your customers. I've been pouring shots since I was a youngin. I got this." I told her, taking Mr. Herman's cup and heading towards the kitchen.

"Make it a double." Mr. Herman called after me.

"Alright. Do you need a soda to mix it with?" I asked, stopping in the doorway to wait for his reply.

"Nah, I already have one." He held up a can of sprite.

"Okay." I turned and continued in the kitchen to get his drink.

After pouring Mr. Herman's drink, I grabbed the cup and was headed back in the den. When there was a tap on the kitchen door. I went over and opened the door. Tre, another of my grandma's regulars, was standing on the other side. I'd seen him quite a few times and we'd conversed on several occasions, but I wouldn't say I knew him like that. He was a few years older than me. Probably in like his mid-thirties. This guy was like a Boykins legend or something. If you were from Boykins, you knew or knew of Tremaine Jefferson. This nigga had really been through some shit. A few years back, one of his baby mama's had been killed in a drive-by, by some niggas trying to kill him. Shortly after that, his other baby mama had driven his kids off a fuckin bridge. People say she did it as some type of payback because he'd been cheating on her with the baby mama that died but after ol girl died, he still didn't want to be with her. She came out of the accident with minor injuries, but the kids got fucked up pretty bad. Then, the crazy bitch left town to avoid going to jail. That left Tre to take care of the two disabled kids and his other two kids that he had with the chick that died. You could look at him and tell, all of that shit had taken a toll on him. He'd always been a slim nigga but he'd loss even more weight and his hair was damn near completely grey. I felt sorry for buddy.

"What's up? Come on in, man." I told him, stepping back out of the way.

"What's up?" He greeted me, as he walked in. "My cousin, Dro coming in behind me."

"Okay. No problem." Just as the words left my mouth, Dro walked up on the porch. I knew Dro from playing basketball together a few times. A lot of guys would get together and play NC against VA from time to time. He and I had played on the same team, a few times. Plus, I knew his baby mama, Keema. She used to fuck with my cousin, Jordan.

"What's up, man?" Dro spoke, walking in.

"What's up?" I replied, closing the door.

"Where's Ms. Lizzie at?" Tre inquired.

"She's in the den."

"Cool." He nodded and proceeded towards the den, with Dro and I behind him.

When we got in the den, I handed Mr. Herman his drink and took a seat in one of the plastic chairs grandma had placed around the room for her customers because the old heads had started a card game at the table.

"What's going on y'all?" Tre asked, walking around and dapping up the fellas at the table and the others that were sitting around talking and watching the card game. Then, he and Dro also took a seat in one of the plastic chairs.

"Hey, y'all." Grandma Lizzie spoke, looking up from what she was doing. "How you been doing, Tre?"

"I've been hanging in there." He replied.

"How's the kids?"

"They're good. Getting big and more worrisome by the day."

Grandma just chuckled.

"They ever catch up with that crazy ass baby mama of yours?" Mr. James, one of the old heads, blurted. That was a dead giveaway that he'd had too many drinks. He never knew what to say out of his mouth once he'd had too many.

"Man, I ain't here to talk about that." Tre replied, an irritated expression covering his face.

I saw Dro give Mr. James a sideways glance and then shake his head. Then, he turned his attention to Grandma Lizzie. "Do you have any Henessey, Ms. Lizzie?"

"Yeah, I believe so. Probably not much, though. I need to go to the liquor store and restock but I don't like going out too much. I know people think this C-19 mess is gone but I don't trust it."

"C-19?" Tre and I questioned, in unison.

"What in the hell is C-19, Lizzie?" Mr. James, asked, laughing. His big belly jiggling as he leaned back laughing like it was the funniest thing he'd ever heard. "It's called Covid-19 and all you have to do is wear a mask when you go out if you're all that scared. I don't even believe that shit is real. I haven't worn no damn mask since they came up with that shit."

"If it ain't real then why so many folks laid out there in the cemetery that had it?" Grandma Lizzie wanted to know.

James took another sip of his drink before replying. "Shit them folks probably didn't die from no Covid. That's just some bullshit the government wants y'all to believe."

"Well, I believe it."

"You believe it but you ain't stopped selling liquor since it started and I ain't seen not one motherfucka come in here with a mask on." Mr. James pointed out. "Let me guess, you think the liquor kills it."

"Did I say that?" Grandma snapped. She hated being wrong about anything and she knew Mr. James had a valid point.

"Well, you said you were scared to go out because of Covid. If you believe it's real, then you should believe that you don't have to go out to get it. Hell, a motherfucka can bring it up in here." He paused and took another sip of his drink. "All I'm saying is, you may as well go out, if you're allowing everyone to come in. You've been fine this long and ain't caught it."

"Nah, I still don't like being out in them stores with folks I don't know. I know the folks that come up in here and I trust them."

"Lizzie, you can catch the shit from a person you know just like you can a stranger. It ain't about who you know or don't know. You're talking stupid."

"Who in the hell are you calling stupid?" Grandma snapped.

"I said what you said was stupid, Lizzie. Calm down."

"I'm calm. You'd better watch your fuckin mouth."

"Alright, Lizzie. I ain't about to argue wit'chu. You know, I love you, girl."

I was glad that one of them had sense enough to let that conversation go.

"Ms. Lizzie, can I get that Hennessy?" Dro asked.

"Yeah, I'm about to get up and go in there."

"I'll get it, grandma. You just get your potatoes." I told her.

"Thanks, Choc. Can you take this bag of peelings in there and throw them in the trash."

"Yeah." I grabbed the bag of peelings off the floor. Then, turned my attention to Dro. "Hey man, do you want a regular shot or a double?"

"A double and a beer. What kind y'all got?"

"I've got a list written on that board in the kitchen." Grandma Lizzie replied. "Go on in the kitchen with Choc and pick what you want."

Dro stood to his feet and so did Tre.

"I'm gonna get a beer, too." Tre announced.

"Alright, come on in the kitchen." I told him and then went into the kitchen.

First, I gave them their beers. Then, I poured Dro and myself a double shot of Henessey. I hadn't come just to play bartender for everyone else. I was trying to enjoy my time away from Brie and our drama. While I was pouring the drinks, grandma came in and began cooking.

"Ms. Lizzie would it be ok if we just sat in here?" Tre asked.

"Yeah, that's fine." She replied and then asked. "Are you still cutting hair?"

"Yeah, I cut at my house most of the time when I'm off from my other job."

"That's good. And what do you do, Dro?"

"I drive trucks." He answered.

"Okay. You are getting that money." Grandma laughed.

"That's what I'm trying to do." I commented.

"Shit, it ain't hard." Dro let me know. "I went right to the community college over in Halifax and took the eight-week course. Best decision, I've made in a while."

"Word? That's in Weldon, NC. Ain't it?"

"Yeah. Go on and get in there, man. I'm telling you. You'll love it. The best part is being to myself and not having nobody breathing down my neck all the time like it was when I was working in warehouses. Plus, the money is good. You just have to grind and not be on no bullshit."

"That's what's up." I nodded. "I'm gonna check that out."

"You sure need to." Grandma butted in. "That job you got at that barbershop can't be paying enough to take care of all of them babies you keep making."

"They are taken care of, though." I let her know, not liking how she had tried to play me in front of company. Sometimes, she didn't know what to say out of her mouth. I think, she picked up on the seriousness in my tone because she didn't say anything else.

I stayed in the kitchen chopping it up and drinking with Tre and Dro for the next few hours. Then, we stepped outside and smoked a blunt. After that I was done!

"Fellas, it's been nice choppin it up with y'all but I'm about to head on out." I told them, running my hands over my face and shaking my head, trying to clear it a little.

"This nigga is done!" Tre laughed.

"For real!" Dro joined in laughing.

I laughed, too, because they were right. "Man, fuck y'all!"

"You good to drive, nigga?" Dro asked.

"Yeah, I'm straight." I replied, unsure.

"Aight, be safe out there on that road and watch out for those damn deer on your way home." Tre told me, sounding just like a damn father.

"Man, I got it. I ain't got that far to go. Just up the street."

"I thought you lived in Franklin?" Dro questioned.

"I do but Franklin won't see me tonight." I laughed and then headed in the direction of my car.

Yaya

Fresh out the shower, dressed in my bathrobe, a towel wrapped around my hair, and a hot mug of chamomile tea. I was seated on my bed with my cell propped up on the nightstand, partaking in my nightly FaceTime call with Ajah and Mari. We'd been on the phone for almost an hour. Neither of them had been able to get a word in edgewise because I'd been venting nonstop about the call, I'd received from Choc earlier.

"Can y'all believe, he had the audacity to call me apologizing after two whole fuckin weeks? Two whole fuckin weeks!" I vented. Without giving them a chance to reply, I continued. "Hmph, this man must take me to the dumbest woman on the fuckin planet."

"Well, maybe not the dumbest but probably close to it." Mari shrugged, taking a sip from the wine glass in her hand.

"Really Mari?" I shot her a nasty look, before rolling my eyes. Sometimes, she and Ajah could be so insensitive to my feelings. I understood the fact that we joked around a lot but damn there was a time to joke and a time to be serious. Right now, in this moment I was serious as a heart attack. "Why can't y'all ever be serious?"

"Wait a minute." Ajah interjected. "Who is y'all? I haven't said a word. I'm just here to be a listening ear because every time I open my mouth, I end up saying the wrong thing."

"Girl, we will always say the wrong thing when it isn't what she wants to hear." Mari sucked her teeth.

"I don't want y'all to say what I want to hear." I exploded, growing frustrated. "I want y'all to be honest with me, but I also want y'all to be serious and stop with all the little wise cracks and shit. I'm hurting for real over here. My feelings aren't a fuckin joke."

"In that case, you need to stop acting like it!" Mari shot back. "No one is taking your feelings for a joke, except Choc. He's the one you need to be upset with for not being serious and for playing games with your feelings. Knowing damn well, he wasn't done playing house with his baby mama."

"Did I say…" I started to speak but was cut-off.

"I'm not done!" Mari snapped, sitting up on her sofa. "Not only do you need to be upset with Choc, but you also need to be upset with yourself. Stop blaming everyone except for you. Take accountability for your part in all of this. Sitting around talking about, you thought you could love him enough to make him change and choose you! That's the dumbest shit, I've ever heard and for some reason women love saying it! You are old enough to know that you can't change a man that doesn't want to change. Come on, now. Stop sitting up here acting like you are some young teenage girl, living in a fantasy world. You are grown grown. Too damn grown to be thinking that how much you love a man or what you do for him will keep him. You and his baby mama accept everything that man does to y'all. Then, y'all want to sit around and cry. It's not like y'all don't know that you're sharing this man. Y'all know about each other! Y'all been knew! So, what's the real problem here? Let me guess. He's giving her more time than you this month. Is that the issue? Or is it that you think she's won this time? I mean, because if that's what you're crying about. Let me go ahead and soothe your little heart. She hasn't won. You said he called. He called because he needed to check and see if you were still stupid, and you gave him the confirmation he needed by answering. I'm willing to bet, he'll be slithering his way back to you, soon. Probably before the week is over. So, with that being said can you please stop whining about Choc's no good ass because I for one am over hearing about him. If I never hear his name again, in this lifetime, it will be too damn soon."

"Well, damn." Ajah erupted with laughter. "Bitch, tell us how you really feel."

Mari sucked her teeth and rolled her eyes. "Girl, I'm just so sick of this mess. Like damn, grow up. Either you gone continue to be that nigga's doormat or you're going to get the fuck up, dust yourself off, and move the fuck on. Plain and fuckin simple!"

I wanted so badly to respond but I couldn't find the words. What could I say? My little sister had sat and read me for filth and not told a single lie. I was so embarrassed, hurt, and frustrated that I hung up. They were tired of hearing about my feelings and I was tired of trying to get them to understand my feelings. Regardless to how they viewed my situation, whether they felt I was stupid or I was completely at fault. It still didn't change the fact that I was hurting and unsure of how to move past all of this. I needed them. Honestly, I felt that I was stupid, too. How could I, an attractive, well-educated, successful woman, allow myself to be in a situation like this? I wasn't a woman with low self-esteem. I didn't have any issues with getting attention from men. Plenty of men hit on me and offered to take me out. Some practically begged for a moment of my time. I'm not talking about no scrubs, either. I'm talking about good looking, successful men. Men who would probably be more than happy to be in a monogamous, healthy relationship with me. So, why had I settled for someone who couldn't even be consistent with something as little as replying to my texts? How had I allowed myself to fall in love with someone who constantly showed me that he wasn't capable of loving me back the way that I loved him?

I sat my tea down on the nightstand and got up from my bed. My mind was in overdrive and my thoughts scrambled. I began pacing back and forth, hoping it would help to clear my head. This shit with Choc had literally consumed me. All I thought about was the past three years. Every single second of our relationship from the day we met played on repeat in my head, day in and day out. I kept replaying everything, trying to figure out where things had gone from sugar to shit because things hadn't always been this way. In the beginning, things were perfect. Choc was everything I'd ever wanted in a man. He was attentive, loving, funny, supportive, and protective. He'd made me feel like the luckiest woman in the world. So, how had I gone from feeling like the luckiest woman to the dumbest woman? Mari's words echoed in my head, *'You and his baby mama accept everything that man does'*. She was right. That's where things had taken a turn for the worse. When I'd found out about Brie and stayed. Yes, he'd lied and swore to me that he was done with her, but I knew better. What woman doesn't know when her man is entertaining someone else? Woman's intuition is a gift and a curse. To keep it real, I'd suspected that he was still involved with Brie before she'd called and told me they were together. I just didn't have proof before she'd called.

I removed the towel from my hair, allowing my damp locs to fall onto my shoulders. Tossing the towel onto the chaise at the end of my bed, I removed my robe and tossed that onto the chaise, as well. I'm not sure if it was all in my head or not but suddenly, I felt hot and uncomfortable. I walked over to my dresser and rummaged through the drawers until I found a pair of pajama shorts and the top to match. After slipping them on, I sat back down and began sipping my tea, my eyes landed on the pic of Choc and I, on my nightstand. In the pic, we were kissing. Keema had taken that pic of us. I loved it so much that I'd printed it out and put it in a frame. Tears rolled down my cheeks. I missed him so much. I felt so broken and alone. I reached up and swiped my tears away. I was so sick of crying. I felt like I'd cried every day for the past two weeks.

The ringing of the doorbell caused me to jump. Wiping my eyes, again, I picked up my phone to check the time and saw that it was a little after ten. *Who in the fuck is at my door?* I thought about Ajah and Mari, but I'd just gotten off the phone with them and they both lived on the outskirts of Boykins. It would've taken them longer than the time we'd been off the phone to get to my house. The doorbell rang, again. Whoever it was, was persistent. I got up and shuffled to the bathroom. Turning on the light, I looked at my reflection in the mirror. I didn't look too crazy, but anyone would be able to see that I'd been crying. I blew my nose and then quickly washed my face. Before I could make it out of the bathroom, the doorbell started to ring, again but this time the person kept ringing it repeatedly.

"This has to be Ajah's and Mari's ass!" I snapped, wondering how and why they were at my door. "I'm coming!" I shouted. A part of me didn't even want to answer the door. I just wanted to be left alone. When, I reached the door, I snatched it open, prepared to give Mari and Ajah a piece of my mind. "Why in the fuck..." My words trailed off when my eyes landed on Choc. I'd wondered how I would feel once I laid eyes on him, again. The only thing I felt in this moment was pain. Seeing him, physically hurt. Standing there staring at him, my heart seemed to be the only organ working properly because my lungs felt like that were about to give out. I felt like, I was fighting to breathe, and my brain had completely shutdown. There'd been so many things that I'd gone over in my head over the past two weeks that I'd wanted to say to him once we were face to face. However, here I was face to face with him and not a single thing that I'd planned to say came to mind. This was the affect that this man had on me.

"Hey. Can I come in?" He asked, his eyes glued to mine. He was 6ft 3inches of midnight chocolate perfection. This man could've easily been a model. His skin was flawless. There wasn't a spec of imperfection on his entire body. God had taken his time on him. Even his dark eyes were captivating. His grandmother often joked that his dark eyes made him appear demonic, but I thought they gave him a sexy, mysterious look.

I couldn't stand the eye contact. So, I looked away and asked. "Choc, what are you doing here?"

"Can I come in?" He slurred, ignoring my question.

The stench of alcohol smacked me in the face. That was my answer as to why he was at my door. He was drunk. "Choc go home." I told him. I didn't want to talk to him in this condition. I preferred to deal with him sober. I attempted to close the door, but he pushed against it, preventing me from closing it. "Choc, stop! You're drunk. Just leave, please! Damn! Just go! Ain't leaving what you're good at?"

"We need to talk. It's a lot of shit you don't know. I understand you're mad but if you would just let me explain. Maybe then you will understand why I did what I did." He pleaded, still pushing against the door.

Growing tired of pushing against him and angry at the same time, I let go of the door and got in his face. "What more do you want from me? I have done everything for you. I have loved you with everything in me, knowing you didn't feel the same. Knowing you had someone else but praying one day you would wake up and choose me because of the way that I love you. I love you unconditionally, flaws and all." I was now pressing against his chest with my index finger with each word that I spoke. "I have accepted you as you are but what has that gotten me? Besides, looking like a damn fool and being left without so much as an explanation! I wasn't even worth a fuckin explanation! I had to be informed by my sister that you'd moved in with Brie and was expecting another baby.

A baby that was conceived while you were running back here fucking me raw, every other night! You have disrespected me and treated me like I am lower than shit on the bottom of your shoe. My heart is broken! I feel like it's been ripped out of my body. I am holding myself together the best I know how because I am so ashamed that I allowed someone to treat me this way. I just want to evaporate into thin fuckin air. So, I won't have to continue walking around feeling and looking stupid. So again, I'm asking you. What in the fuck do you want? Did you come back for my fuckin soul because you've already taken my dignity and self-respect."

"I left for my kids, Ya. They needed me. So, I left to be there for them." He tried to explain but I wasn't trying to hear it.

"That's bullshit! Don't blame this shit on those kids. Be a man! Tell me the truth. You chose her! Just say that!" Without thinking, I drew back and slapped him hard across the face and then started hitting him in his chest with my fists. "Say it! Say, you chose her over me! Say, I've never been enough for you! Say it, Choc! Tell me, I've only been a fill-in for when you're mad at her and shit ain't going your way over there! Say, I'm the one you come to when you need your ego stroked and your wounds licked because I'm the dumb ass always here to build you up when everyone else is tearing you down! Me! I'm the mothafucka always rooting for you and believing in you even when you don't believe in yourself."

"Yaya, stop!" He grabbed me by both arms and pushed me inside, closing the door with his foot. All the while, I was fighting against him, trying to free my arms.

"Get off of me! Get the fuck off of me!" I screamed through tears. "I fuckin hate you! How could you do me like this? Why would you string me along, knowing you didn't want me? What kind of person does shit like that?"

"Ya, it wasn't like that, baby. I swear! If you would just calm the fuck down and listen to me."

"Listen for what? So, that you can just stand here and continue lying to my face?"

In an instant, his expression changed. He brought his face close to mine and screamed. "I'm not lying. How many fuckin times do I have to tell your ass that? You're starting to piss me off because you keep running your fuckin mouth but you ain't listening to shit, I say. Shut the fuck up and listen!"

"Fuck you! I'm not gonna listen to shit you have to say. So, you can take your triflin ass back to Franklin to your baby mama and your kids. Brie can have you because

114

Iyanna don't need you!" I spat and then tried to snatch away from his grasp, but he snatched me back to him.

"I said shut the fuck up and listen." He spoke through clenched teeth. "Do you honestly think I would've driven over here if I didn't give a fuck about you or if I had chosen Brie and shit was all lovely over there with her? Do you think I would've called and apologized to your ass if I didn't give a fuck about you or your feelings?" He paused as if he was waiting for a response, but I couldn't reply because the water works had come on, again. I wanted to kick myself in the ass for crying in front of him like this and appearing so weak, but I couldn't help it. "She overdosed a little while ago and her mom threatened to take the kids if we didn't get our shit together and put them in a suitable home. I thought about taking my kids, leaving Brie, and settling down with you. I mean, I really considered it. I knew without a doubt that you would accept my kids and love them as your own. Even the one that's on the way. I knew you would be mad once you found out about the new baby, but I knew that you would still accept it because of your love for me. Choosing you would've been easier. Hell, it probably would've been what was best for the kids, but I couldn't bring myself to do Brie like that."

Soon as those words left his lips, I was done listening. "But you could do me like that!" I tried to snatch away, again.

Again, he snatched me back to him.

"I said shut the fuck up and listen." He barked. "She's sick. She has been for a long time. She suffers from depression, and she has a drug addiction. She started fuckin with drugs a few years back. She's overdosed twice. She needs help. She's been to rehab but honestly, I don't know how long that will work. I mean, she went before and started back using, again. So, I'm not really convinced this time will be different. Especially since, she only stayed for a month. I feel like it may help short term, but I don't know about in the long run. I'm just hoping that it does because the kids need for her to get better."

"And you. You need for her to get better because if she does. Y'all can run off into the sunset together. While I'm left looking like the dumb ass that wasted three years of my life, waiting for a man to choose me."

He finally let go of me and let out a frustrated breath. "Stop saying that shit. It wasn't a waste of time! I love you but she needs me. My fuckin kids need me! If I had chosen, you and turned my back on her. What kind of nigga would that make me? How could I be good laying up here with you, while my kid's mother is doing drugs and my kids are living with their grandparents?"

"You're making excuses. You could've gotten a place of your own and taken your kids from her. That's what would've been best. You staying with her won't fix her and you know that just like I do. So, don't feed me some bullshit about you choosing her because she's sick and needs you. You chose her because you love her. Don't stand here and play me like I'm stupid!"

"I'm not playing you! I'm telling you the truth."

"Bullshit! Like you said, she's been sick for a while. Why haven't you been trying to get her some professional help? Why would you just keep fucking her and get her pregnant, again? Let me guess. You thought, your dick could cure her?"

"Fuck! Why can't you at least try and understand what I'm saying?"

"Because you're full of shit. I mean, it sounds good but it's bullshit. This isn't all about her depression or her drug habit. No one would choose to move in with or impregnate someone in an attempt to fix their mental health. Do I really look that stupid?"

"Yes, I love her. You already know that but that's not why, I got the apartment with her. I got that place for my kids and to try and keep them with me and their mother. They are our kids. We should be raising them not their grandparents."

By now, I was tired of going back and forth. I felt like we were talking in circles and not accomplishing anything. Discussing this wasn't making me feel any better. As a matter of fact, it was making me feel worse. At this point, I just wanted him to leave. So, that I could be alone. "Look, it doesn't matter. You've made your decision and it is what it is."

"It does matter. I didn't want to hurt you."

"Well, you did but I guess it was for a good cause. According to you."

He walked over and took a seat on the sofa, placing his head in his hands. He looked stressed out and defeated. Sadly, I felt sorry for him. Even though, this was a mess that he'd created. I felt bad. "This shit is so fuckin confusing. I'm trying to do the right thing, but I can't stop thinking about you. I miss you. I love you and I don't want to lose you. I don't want you fuckin with another nigga."

I let out a chuckle, shaking my head. "You're so fuckin selfish." I scoffed.

"How am I selfish because I don't want you fuckin with some other nigga?"

"Aren't you living with and in a relationship with your baby mama?"

"A relationship? Yeah, if that's what you want to call it." He mumbled. "I'm more like her caregiver."

"Well, whatever, *y'all* want to call it. You need to focus on your family, not who I may or not fuck with."

He sprang to his feet, closing the space between us with one giant step. "Yaya don't play with me. I will fuck you up."

"Boy, move." I pushed him away, rolling my eyes. "You have who you want. So, like I said, focus on your family."

"I don't have who I want because I want you, too." He admitted, pushing me back against the wall, and covering my lips with his.

Just the feel of his lips against mine, began to instantly diminish my anger. I pushed him away, again. "Choc, go home."

He pulled me into him and kissed me, again. Against my better judgment, I kissed him back. This time, we kissed passionately. I wanted to push him away again, but I couldn't. My body wouldn't allow it because my body craved him. After all of this, my body still craved him. My heart still wanted him. Even with my brain screaming, *stop...don't do this.* My heart held the deciding vote. My arms found their way up around his neck and his found their way around my waist, pulling me in closer to him, as our tongues made love to each other. *God, I'd missed him.*

He pulled back momentarily and whispered. "I love you, Ya."

"I love you, too." I whispered back, looking him directly in his eyes. I always looked him in his eyes whenever I expressed my feelings because I wanted him to know I meant it.

He picked me up and carried me down the hallway to my bedroom. Inside the bedroom, we ripped off our clothes in record time, and climbed onto the bed. He was on top of me, between my thighs, kissing the insides of them. As I lay back enjoying the feel of his lips on my skin, I couldn't help but think of the last time we were together. My brain kept shouting, *bitch, get up!* I knew how this was going to end. He was going to fuck me good and go back to her and I'd be left feeling even dumber than before. I had to stop this.

I opened my mouth to tell him to stop and at the same time, he wrapped his lips around my clit, silencing me. *Fuck!* His mouth felt so good, my entire body shuttered beneath him, as he expertly licked and sucked on my clit. I closed my eyes and bit down on my lip, feeling my orgasm building. I didn't want to cum too quickly, but I knew it was inevitable. Especially when I felt him slip his fingers inside of me and began working them in and out, while continuing his assault on my clit.

"Oh, shit! Oh shit! Ooooo God!" I shouted, cumming so hard that I nearly passed out. I tried to scoot back away from his tongue while using my hands to push his head back, but he hooked his arms around my thighs, holding me in place. "Choc, please stop!" I begged.

Giving my clit, one last kiss. He released me and laughed. "You should be used to this tongue by now. What are you running for?"

"Because you play too much."

"You just be tasting so good. I don't be wanting to stop." He said, kissing a trail from my stomach to my lips.

As we kissed, I felt the head of his manhood searching for my opening. Again, my conscience spoke up. *Don't do it, Yaya. What is this gonna change?* That was a good question. What would it change, except for making me feel worse when it was over? Were a few minutes of pleasure worth making an already fucked up situation worse? A degrading feeling came over me and I became instantly disgusted with myself.

"Stop!" I demanded, just as he found my opening and slid inside. I pushed against his chest and at the same time, tried to sit up. "Stop Choc. Get off of me. I don't want to do this, anymore."

He stopped and looked down at me. His face wrinkled with confusion. "What? Are you serious?"

"Yes. Now, move." I replied, still trying to push him up off of me.

"What the fuck, yo?" He huffed, getting up.

I got up, too, and grabbed my robe from the chaise. "I'm sorry but I just can't. Us fucking won't change shit. It'll just make shit worse." I explained, while pulling on my robe and tying it.

"Whatever, yo." He replied, putting on his clothes. "First, you want to fuck, now you don't. You got me in here feeling like I'm taking advantage of you or some shit. Like, I'm on some rapist type shit. Talking about, stop get off of you. This shit right here is crazy."

"I agree it is, but I never said anything about you being a rapist or taking advantage of me. You're dragging it." I corrected him, while shaking my head. Letting out a sigh, I continued. "I can't keep on forgiving you and jumping back in bed with you. Then, feel some type of way when you go back to Brie. It has to stop. I can't do this no more. You've made your choice. Now, stand on it."

"I explained that shit to you!" He barked, getting up in my face. "I told you, I went back for my kids."

"The point is, you went back! So, stay there and stop running back to me! I'm not a fuckin toy that you can play with and then toss me aside when you're done! I deserve better than that! Stop feeling like you can just walk in and out of my life when you feel like it! Like you said earlier about you knowing I would accept the new baby because of how much I love you. That's the problem, you feel, I will accept anything because I love you. What about me? Don't I deserve that same type of love?"

"I do love you!"

"Not the way I deserve to be loved!" I screamed so loudly that it hurt my throat. Trembling with anger and my eyes locked on his. I spoke from my soul. "I deserve more than some half ass love and a man that I have to share. I'm done! Go home, Choc. Go back to your family that you are supposedly trying so hard to do right by. I'm sure fucking me ain't a part of you doing right by Brie."

"Man, I'm out." He brushed past me, bumping my shoulder so hard that I stumbled backwards. "You ain't gotta worry about me no more."

123

"That's the plan." I yelled after him.

He didn't reply. He kept walking and a few seconds later, I heard the front door slam. I went down the hall and locked the door. Then, turned off all the lights in the front part of the house and went back into my room. Back in my room, I flopped down on the bed. I couldn't believe what had just taken place. I couldn't believe, I'd had the strength to say no to Choc. I was proud of myself and at the same time, afraid. Afraid that I'd lost him for good because honestly, I did want things to be different. I still wanted him to choose me and for us to live happily ever after. That's what I wanted but the reality of the situation was, I couldn't keep doing the same shit when it came to him and expecting different results. So, if I had lost him for good, at least I could be proud of the fact that this time, I'd done the right thing. Lord knows, I'd done enough of the wrong things.

****

Over the next few weeks, I mostly just went to work and straight back home. I didn't feel like being bothered with anyone. I just wanted to be by myself to deal with everything that had recently transpired between Choc and I. I was hurting real bad about having to let him go but I knew I was making the right decision. I couldn't keep breaking my own heart or hurting my own feelings and blaming everyone else. It was time to put on my big girl panties and take some accountability for my own actions. I'd explained to Ajah and Mari that I needed some space. They understood and didn't trip about it.

After three weeks of being inside, I'd began growing bored and felt the need for a little fresh air. Still not wanting to be bothered with anyone. I decided to get dressed and take myself on a little solo date. Being that it was a Saturday night, and I was off the next day, I decided to go to the Mexican restaurant out in Franklin for dinner and drinks. I got dressed in a cute little floral two-piece skirt set and a pair of wedge sandals. I did a little light natural beat on my face, put on some lip gloss, pulled my locs back into a ponytail, and threw on some medium sized gold hoops. I checked my reflection in the mirror and was pleased with the results. So, I grabbed my cell, purse and keys and was headed out the door. Just as I got to the door, my cell began to ring. I checked to see who was calling and saw Ajah's name flashing on the screen. I answered and pressed the phone against my ear.

"Hey girl."

"Hey chick. What you up to? I haven't talked to you today and wanted to check up on you." Ajah replied.

"I'm good. I'm on my way out to get a little fresh air. Tired of being cooped up in the house."

"Oh ok. Well, that's good. Where are you headed?"

"Just to Franklin to grab something to eat and maybe a little drink."

"Okay. Well, I'm glad you're getting out. Hopefully you'll bump into a fine piece of dark chocolate while you're out." She giggled.

I laughed too. "Girl, bye. The last thing on my mind is a man."

"Shit, it needs to be the first. You know what they say. The best way to get over one man is to get under or on top of another one. Whichever you prefer."

We both burst into laughter.

"Girl, you ain't got one ounce of sense." I told her.

"I'm for real! Shit, ain't no need to sit around sad and crying over the past when it ain't sitting around sad or crying over you. Out with the old and in with the new. And by new, I mean get you some new dick to help you get over the old one."

"Bye, Ajah. I'm about to go get me something to eat. I'll call you later."

"Not you trying to rush me off the phone but bye. Enjoy yourself."

"Alright." I ended the call and continued out the door.

When I arrived at El Rancheros, they were packed. Seeing so many cars in the parking lot, a nervous feeling formed in the pit of my stomach. I didn't want to bump into Choc and Brie. That was the last thing I needed. Especially, when I was just starting to feel a little bit better. *I'm here, now. So, I may as well get out and try to enjoy myself.* I gave myself a mental pep talk, while opening my car door and getting out. I went inside and was greeted by the hostess.

"Good evening. How many?" She asked.

"Just me."

"Do you prefer a booth or table? Or would you like to have a seat at the bar?"

"I can sit at the bar." I told her.

"Okay, that's fine."

I walked over to the bar and took a seat. Soon as my ass touched the seat the bartender asked what I wanted to drink. I ordered a top shelf margarita. While, I waited for my drink, I looked around, observing the crowd. They had a nice mixed crowd. Everyone seem to be enjoying themselves with friends and family. That made me miss Ajah and Mari a little but me knowing that if they were there, I would get drunk and bring up Choc. I knew me being solo was best. I didn't feel like arguing with them about how I felt anymore. I wanted to be free to feel how I felt and heal in my own way. If I wanted to cry every day until the pain was gone. I wanted to do that with no judgment. I knew eventually I would be okay. I just needed to thug this shit out in my own way.

The bartender placed my drink down in front of me and then asked if I wanted to order food or an appetizer.

"Yes, I'd like to order some fresh guacamole with chips, please." I replied, giving him a polite smile. He was a cutie, dark hair, bronze complexion, gorgeous smile but a little too short for my taste.

"I'll put that in for you." He told me, returning the same polite smile. Then, left to go put in my order.

I pulled out my phone and opened up Instagram and began strolling, while sipping my drink.

"We've gotta stop bumping into each other at restaurants like this." I heard a male voice say.

I turned to my right and saw Dro standing next to me, wearing a huge smile. "Hey." I blushed, inhaling the intoxicating scent of his cologne. He smelled good enough to eat. He was dressed in a white tee, black shorts and black/white Jordans. The gold jewelry he had on complimented his dark complexion. He resembled the rapper Big Boogie a little. *This man is too fine.* I thought to myself. Ajah's words immediately came to mind. You know what they say. *The best way to get over one man is to get under or on top of another one.* I knew I shouldn't be thinking that way because of him being Keema's son father but how could I not with him standing next to me looking like a midnight chocolate God. My weakness had always been dark skinned men. That had been my initial attraction to Choc, his dark complexion. In my opinion, they were the sexiest men God had created and he'd definitely taken his time on Dro. From his skin to his smile to his build. He was fuckin perfection.

"What's up, beautiful? I see you love food just as much as me." He laughed.

"Well, a woman has to eat, right?" I asked, taking another sip of my drink.

"That's true." He nodded and pointed to the empty barstool next to me. "Is anyone sitting here?"

"Nah."

"Do you mind if I sit next to you?"

"Not at all."

He slid onto the barstool next to me and asked. "What's that you're drinking on?"

"A top shelf margarita." I replied, laying my phone down on the bar.

"Oh ok. I think, I'm gonna need something a little stronger than that."

"I can't handle anything much stronger than this. I'm driving. Don't want to end up in the ditch or hitting a deer. You know, deer be jumping out everywhere down my way."

"Yeah, I just left B-Town. I was out there visiting my cousin, Tre." He informed me.

"Tremaine Jefferson?" I asked, with raised eyebrows.

"Yeah. Do you know him?"

"Kinda sorta. His baby mama Lala was my cousin."

"Oh damn." A sympathetic expression took over his face. "Sorry for your loss."

"Thanks."

"It's a small world, huh?"

"Yeah, it is." I nodded, taking another sip of my margarita. Not liking the sympathetic look he was giving me, I made an attempt to lighten the mood. "Guess this kinda makes us sorta like family, doesn't it?"

"Oh naw!" He replied without hesitation, while shaking his head.

"Oh you don't want to be my cousin?" I giggled, eyeing him. I couldn't seem to tear my eyes away from him. I was trying not to stare but he oozed sex appeal or maybe it was the fact that I hadn't had any in a few weeks. Either way, being in his presence was having an arousing affect on me.

"No disrespect but hell naw!" He laughed. "Naw, we definitely can't be cousins." His eyes roamed down to the short skirt I was wearing then back up to my face. He shook his head again. "Naw, definitely not."

I couldn't stop laughing at his forwardness. The little bit of margarita I had consumed had me feeling a little tipsy already. The bartender had made it kinda strong but I wasn't complaining. I felt good. "I wonder why." I replied, licking my lips.

Before, Dro could respond, the bartender returned and sat my guacamole and chips down in front of me. "Here you are ma'am."

"Thank you."

"Would you like to order anything to drink or eat?" He asked Dro.

"Yeah, let me get a shot of Patron and Corona. Can I also get an order of wings?"

"Yes sir, you can. I'll get those wings in for you and be right back with that shot of Patron and Corona."

"Preciate that, my man." Dro replied.

"Want some?" I offered, picking up a chip and dipping it in the guacamole.

"Ugh-uhh. I don't like the way it looks. I can't get past the color or texture." He admitted, twisting up his face. "But I appreciate the offer."

"Suit yourself but it's good." I shrugged, before beginning to enjoy my appetizer.

"I'll take your word for it." Dro chuckled.

The bartender returned and placed Dro's drinks in front of him. "Those wings will be out shortly." He said before walking away.

Dro picked up his drink and took a sip. Then, picked up his beer and took a long swig. "So, what are you doing here all alone, looking all beautiful? Where's your man?"

That question caught me off-guard and shifted my entire mood. I picked up my drink and took a big gulp. Dro must've picked up on my uneasiness.

"You don't have to answer, if you don't want to. Looks like my question may have struck a nerve."

I took another gulp of my drink before answering. "Nah, it's cool. I don't mind answering. He's with his baby mama." I told him, matter-of-factly.

Looking at me, wearing a confused expression. He said, "Come again. He's where?"

"With his baby mama." I repeated.

"Are you serious or being funny?"

"Shit, I wish I was being funny but unfortunately. I'm dead serious. Wasted three years, loving and catering to a man, for him to pick up and leave to go back to his baby mama." I said, somberly. I hadn't meant to blurt my personal business out like that but it was out, now. The miserable feeling, I'd been feeling for the past few weeks returned and instantly, I was ready to go.

Dro shook his head. "Damn, that's tough. That nigga done messed it up for all niggas with baby mamas. You want me to go whoop his ass?"

I hadn't expected that response. "What?"

"You heard what I asked you. Do you want me to go whoop that nigga's ass?"

"Now, why would you do that for me?" I laughed.

"I'll be doing it for both of us because he hurt you and because he ruined my chance."

"Ruined your chance? Who said you had a chance?"

"I was hoping, I did." Dro looked at me. His gaze was lustful but there was something more than lust in his eyes. He was feeling me and it showed. I remembered that same look being in his eyes when I'd seen him at Cracker Barrel, a few weeks prior. Between my attraction to him and his obvious attraction to me, he had me ready to take it there with him. Throw caution to the wind and enjoy a night of fun with no strings attached but I knew it would be foul of me to deal with him on any level due to the fact that he had a baby with Keema. Honestly, I wasn't even sure if I was ready to deal with anyone on any level after all that had recently transpired between Choc and I. I just knew that I felt lonely and missed the touch of a man. Not just any man. I missed Choc's touch and the affection that he showed when we were together, but I also knew that I had to let that go. I had to let him go and accept the fact that he'd chosen Brie and not me.

"I'm flattered but you have a child with my friend. So, that actually deads any chance if there was one."

"Lord have mercy!" Dro laughed. "Now, I want to whoop both their asses!"

"What? Why?"

"Because now she's blocking my chance."

I shook my head and took another sip of my drink. "You're funny."

"Yeah, but I'm serious." He said, staring at me for a moment, before downing the rest of his Patron.

The bartender returned and placed Dro's wings down in front of him. "Is there anything else I can get for either of you?"

"No, I'm fine." I told him.

"Yeah, I'm straight." Dro replied. Then turned to me and asked. "Would you like some?"

"Nah, I don't eat chicken." I declined.

"You don't eat chicken?"

"Nah. I'm pescatarian. I gave up poultry, pork, and red meat, years ago."

"Wow. I don't think I've ever met anyone black who doesn't eat chicken." He admitted, biting into a flat.

"There's plenty of black vegans, pescatarians, and vegetarians." I informed him, while taking a sip of my drink.

"I'll take your word for it. I don't know any but I think having that type of discipline is dope."

"For me, it started out as a thirty-day challenge and then became a lifestyle. I liked how I felt during those thirty days. I had more energy and my skin looked better. So, I kept it up." I explained.

"I can dig it." He nodded. "It's definitely working for you because you look damn good. I couldn't believe you were thirty-seven when I saw your recent birthday photos on your page. You don't look a day over twenty-five."

"Thank you."

"So, you're really not going to let me take you out and show you a good time because of Keema?" He asked, not giving up easily.

I shook my head. "Nah, it wouldn't be right." My mouth was saying no but my mind and body were curious.

"Why? She and I have been over for years. She does what wants and I do what I want. The only communication between us is when we discuss DJ. That's it."

"I understand that, but it still wouldn't be right."

"Okay. I won't pressure you, but you shouldn't let that stop you from getting to know me. I could be the man of your dreams."

"Is that right?" I chuckled.

"Yeah."

I decided it was time for me to end the night because if I didn't, I might not be able to keep saying no to him. I looked up in search of the bartender but didn't see him. "I wonder where the bartender disappeared to? I need my check." I said out loud, still looking around.

"You about to go?" Dro looked disappointed.

"Yeah, before I end up doing something I might regret." I confessed, then paused. I hesitated for a second before speaking my thoughts. "You're a hard man to resist. You're very attractive, funny and you smell good as hell, but I have enough drama in my life, and I don't want to add to that by dealing with you. I know, you say that you and Keema are done, and I believe you because she's said the same. However, y'all being done doesn't mean she won't feel some type of way if we start getting to know each other."

"I honestly don't give a damn about how she feels but I respect you. So, I won't come at you like that anymore."

"I appreciate that." I smiled.

"So does that mean, you'll stay and have another drink with me?" Dro asked, giving me his best pouting face.

Against my better judgment, I nodded my head. "I'll only stay if you fix your face and promise to not ever do that again." I giggled, rolling my eyes.

"Bet."

Choc

"Omg, I am starving!" Brie exclaimed from the passenger seat while rubbing her belly. "I can already taste the food. I'm getting the steak and chicken nachos supreme, some fresh guacamole, an order of wings and a virgin strawberry daiquiri." She called out her order, as if she was paying.

"I don't know who's going to pay for all of that." I half joked, wondering why she was talking about ordering the whole menu. When I'd told her that I didn't have a lot of spending money and I wasn't trying to touch what I'd put in my savings. The only reason we were out now was because I was tired of hearing her complain nonstop about being cooped up in the house. I figured taking her out to dinner and getting her out of the house for a few hours would buy me a few days of peace at home.

"You're going to pay for it." She laughed, smacking me playfully on the arm. Then, she began rubbing her belly, again. Her chocolate brown eyes were fixed on me, and a smirk played on her full lips. "This little boy right here loves to eat. Just like his big-headed daddy."

I glanced back at the road then back at her momentarily, taking a moment to really look at her. Before returning my attention to the road. She looked so beautiful pregnant. She'd started to put on some weight, and it looked great on her. Her face was rounder and fuller. She looked healthy. Her hair was getting fuller, and her skin possessed that pregnancy glow. She looked like *my* Brie. The Brie, that I'd fallen in love with. The Brie, before the drugs. I missed that, Brie. Tonight, she'd taken the time to do her makeup and curl her shoulder length hair. I loved it when she wore her hair down in curls because usually, she just pulled it back into a ponytail. She'd even taken the time to put on a cute little dress. I was really feeling her look tonight.

"What was that look about?" Brie questioned.

"Nothing. I was just appreciating your beauty." I admitted, glancing over at her. "You look really beautiful tonight, baby."

"Thanks bae." She blushed.

"You're welcome."

Reaching over and rubbing my thigh, Brie said. "Ooh I like the way this night is starting!"

"Good." I smiled, glad to finally see a smile on her face.

When we got to El Rancheros, I noticed the parking lot was full. I wasn't surprised being that it was Saturday.

Plus, there wasn't a lot to choose from in Franklin as far as places to eat and their food was some of the best in town.

"I hope we can get a table because I don't want to go to Don Panchos. Their food isn't as good, and they don't have a lot to choose from on their menu. El Rancheros definitely has a better menu." Brie stated as I helped her out of the car. "And I damn sure don't want no Applebees. I'd rather not eat."

"I'm sure we'll be able to get a table and if not, we could sit at the bar."

"Boy, I am five and a half months pregnant. I'm not trying to be sitting up at no bar. I want a table or booth so that I can be comfortable. I prefer a booth. So, that I can have some comfortable support against my back. Instead of, one of those hard wooden chairs."

"I'll see if I can get us a booth." I assured her, holding the door for her as we entered.

Once inside, we were greeted by the hostess. "Hello. How many?"

"Two." I replied.

The hostess looked down at the seating chart and then back up at us. "Booth or table?"

"Booth." Brie spoke up, before I could respond.

After grabbing some silverware and menus, the hostess instructed us to follow him to our booth. We did as we were told and followed him through the crowded restaurant. He seated us in a booth a few feet away from the bar.

"Is this ok?"

Brie looked around with her nose turned up, as she slid into the booth. "It's a little loud, sitting right here at the bar filled with loud mouthed drunks but it'll do, I guess." She sucked her teeth, while making a face. "And they all up in my damn face."

"I can sit on the side facing the bar." I offered.

"Nah, it's okay."

"Sorry, ma'am. It's the only booth we have available." The hostess apologized.

"It's fine, man. We appreciate it." I told him.

"Good. Your server will be with you shortly." He smiled and then walked away.

"I can already tell, I'm going to get irritated." Brie huffed, leaning back against the booth with a million wrinkles decorating her face.

"Brie, don't start. I offered to switch seats with you. You didn't want to. You wanted to get out of the house. So now, you're out of the house and you're still complaining." I shook my head. "Can't do shit to please you."

"You should be complaining, too. This is the worst spot in the entire place. They shouldn't give this booth to anyone. How are we supposed to engage in a conversation with all of this noise? We basically have to scream to hear each other."

"Didn't you say you wanted a booth so that you could be comfortable? You have a booth. It may not be perfect but damn at least try to work with what we have and enjoy yourself. That's all I'm saying." She was starting to make me regret trying to appease her. This was one of the things I hated most about her. Nothing was ever enough. I wanted to think it was her hormones making her act this way because of the pregnancy but I knew that wasn't the case. She was this way when she wasn't pregnant.

Smoothing out the wrinkles in her face, she sat up straight, and held her hands up in surrender. "Aight. You got it. I'm gonna chill out."

"Good."

A dark haired, middle-aged, Mexican woman approached our booth. "Hello, I'm your server. What would you like to drink?" She greeted us with a welcoming smile.

"I'll have a virgin strawberry daiquiri with extra whip cream and a glass of water with lemon." Brie answered, then added. "Can I get a few extra lemon slices in a dish, please?"

"Yes, ma'am. And for you sir?"

"I'll have water with lemon."

"Okay. Do you all already know what you would like to order or do you need a few minutes?"

"We already know what we want." I told him and then nodded at Brie. "You can go ahead and order yours first."

"I'll have the steak and chicken nachos supreme, an order of wings with the bone in, and an order of fresh guacamole." Brie called out her order.

The waitress jotted everything down and then looked at me.

"I'll…"

"Oooh and can I get a bowl of the shrimp soup." Brie interrupted, cutting me off. "I haven't had that in so long. I know this is about to be so freakin good. I can't wait!" She folded her menu and placed it down on the table.

The waitress jotted her shrimp soup down and then looked at me again for my order.

Letting out a frustrated sigh, I told her. "I'll have the chicken enchiladas."

"Will that be all?" The waitress asked.

"Yeah." I folded my menu, placed it on top of Brie's and handed them both to the waitress.

"Thank you, sir. I'll go and put those orders in for you." She smiled politely before disappearing towards the kitchen.

"Damn, she all in your face like I'm not sitting here. I hope her old ass don't make me cuss her out." Brie snapped. "All that damn smiling. She wasn't smiling at me like that."

"If you don't chill the fuck out. I'm leaving. I'm not about to sit here and listen to you complain all night. We could've stayed at home." I let her know.

"So, I'm not supposed to speak up when I feel disrespected?" Brie questioned.

Not bothering to respond to her ignorant question. I repeated. "If you are don't chill the fuck out. I'm leaving. Simple as that. Take it however you want to." I looked around and saw people looking in our direction. I took a deep breath and tried to calm myself before continuing. "I'm trying but I can't try by myself. You have to meet me halfway. I know, I'm doing this for you but it's not all about you. I would like to enjoy myself, too."

Brie didn't respond but I could tell by the expression on her face, she didn't like what I'd said.

The waitress returned with our drinks, Brie's guacamole, and the shrimp soup. She placed everything down on the table and let us know that our food would be out shortly.

"You want some?" Brie offered me some of her food.

"Nah."

"Why?"

"I just don't."

Brie didn't say anything. Instead, she began eating her appetizer and looking around. I took out my phone and began strolling on instagram.

"Uggh, I knew I was gonna see somebody I didn't wanna see." Brie hissed, causing me to look up. She dropped the spoon in her soup. Soup splashing onto the table. Wrinkles of frustration decorated her forehead as she stared past me, shaking her head. "The sight of that hoe done turned my fuckin stomach. Probably sitting over there with somebody else's man."

"Who?" I asked, looking around, trying to find who she was talking about.

"*Your bitch!*" She nodded past me.

I turned and saw Yaya seated at the bar with Dro. They were eating and carrying on a conversation. *What the fuck? How does she know him? Is this the reason she's on her strong woman, she doesn't need me shit now?* Brie's voice interrupted my thoughts.

"Damn, you staring like you want to go over there!" She snapped. "Yo, triflin ass probably do. Probably still been sneaking around behind my back wit the bitch."

I turned back around to face Brie. "What? What are you talking about? I hadn't even seen that girl until you said something. So, why the fuck you poppin off at me?" I asked, confused by her attitude.

"You know what? I'm ready to go. Take me home."

"So now you mad and ready to go? All because that girl is here? And she's wit a nigga at that! That girl ain't thinking about us. I bet she wouldn't leave if she saw you. So, why are you so bothered by her?"

An angered expression took over Brie's face and a demonic look danced in her eyes. Jumping to her feet, she leaned over the table and pointed her index finger in my face. "Motherfucka don't you ever in your black ass life

147

assume that your cum drinking, side bitch, got me bothered. That bitch couldn't bother me on my worse day. Why the fuck would I be bothered when you chose me over that bitch? I got what that bitch wants. You got me all the way fucked up! Talking about that bitch or any other bitch got me bothered."

It felt like the entire restaurant was staring at us. I looked around and saw people whispering and pointing in our direction. Standing to my feet, I looked around for our waitress. I spotted her at another table. I walked over to where she was. First, I said excuse me and apologized to the couple she was serving. Then, I turned my attention to her. "I apologize for disturbing you, but we have an emergency and need to leave. Can I please pay for our food and get it to-go?"

"Yes sir, I'll get your check and your food as soon as I'm done here." She told me.

"Thank you." When I turned around Brie was standing behind me.

"Give me the keys! I'm going to the car." She snapped with one hand on her hip and the other hand out waiting on the keys.

I brushed past her and headed back to our booth to wait on the waitress. On my way, I glanced over at Yaya and Dro. They were still engaged in conversation, laughing like they were at a fuckin comedy show. My blood was boiling. I wanted to go over and drag Yaya out by her fuckin neck. I couldn't believe she had the audacity to be out with another nigga just two weeks after she'd done all that crying like she was so hurt about me being with Brie. Looked to me like, she'd healed pretty quickly. She didn't look hurt at all to me. Every time, I looked in her direction, her teeth were showing.

"Give me the fuckin keys!" Brie shouted, now standing next to the booth.

I looked up at her, trying my best not to lose my temper. My eyes went down to her stomach before going back up to her face. "I'm not giving you shit. So, sit down and wait for the waitress to bring the check and food. Then, we can go."

"I'm not..." Brie began but I cut her off.

"Brie, sit down." I demanded through clenched teeth. I was exercising every bit of self-restraint I had.

I don't know if God intervened or common sense kicked in but Brie flopped down in her seat across from me. "Fine. I'll wait but this shit ain't over with." She threatened.

I ignored her threat because honestly, she didn't even have a reason to be upset. She just wanted a reason to continue showing her ass like she'd been doing the entire night. I wasn't about to feed into her bullshit now or when we got home. To be honest, if anyone should be upset it should be me. If I hadn't tried to do the right thing by choosing her over Yaya, none of this would be happening right now. I'd be with Yaya, not having to deal with Brie's constant nagging and complaining. And most importantly, Yaya wouldn't be across the room grinning all up in Dro's face. I'd often wondered how it would feel to see Yaya with someone else. I'd known that I'd probably be pissed but what I mostly felt in this moment was hurt, regret, and jealousy. But who did I have to blame, besides myself?

"Here you are, sir." The waitress handed me the check while placing the to-go bag, containing our food, on the table.

I reached in my pocket, took out my debit card and handed it to the waitress.

"I'll go and take care of this for you. Then, I'll be right back." The waitress assured me before disappearing across the restaurant.

There was complete silence at the table while we waited for the waitress to return. Brie sat across the table with her eyes locked on me, rolling them every time I made eye contact with her. I knew, she was trying to get a reaction out of me but she wasn't going to get it.

The waitress returned shortly with my receipt and debit card. After signing the merchant receipt, I grabbed the bag of food from the table and started out of the restaurant. Soon as we got outside, Brie started up again.

"You so mad about seeing that bitch with another nigga that you just gone leave without telling me to come on, right?" She questioned, waddling behind me as fast as she could in an attempt to keep up with me.

"I figured when I got up to leave, you would have sense enough to get up and follow. Apparently, I was right." I replied, sarcastically. Reaching the car, I pointed the keychain remote at the car and unlocked the doors. I opened the back door and placed the food in the backseat. Before, getting in the driver's seat. Brie was already seated in the passenger seat, still running off at the mouth. I started the car and drove out of the parking lot. Reaching over, I turned up the radio to drown out Brie's pointless rant. I swear, she was proving to be more and more mentally unstable. She was outright delusional. She'd been going on and on for the past few minutes about how I wasn't going to keep disrespecting her and making her look stupid.

I turned down the radio. "How did I disrespect you or make you look stupid?" I asked, not really wanting an answer from her. So, I didn't wait for one. "How the hell do I have control over who comes to a public place? What you think, I called her up and asked her to meet up for a double date? Tell me if that makes logical sense to you because it sure as hell doesn't make sense to me. Do you think I actually wanted to see her with another nigga?" The moment those words left my lips, I knew shit was about to get real but it'd been said and I couldn't take it back.

"Mothafucka! What did you say?" Brie unsnapped her seatbelt and turned in her seat to face me. Without warning, she slapped me right in the center of my face. "I knew you still wanted that bitch!" She slapped me, again.

I nearly lost control of the car. Swerving out of and then back into my lane. I finally regained control of the car and pulled over. All the while, Brie continued her attack as she called me every name she could think of. I put the car in park and grabbed a hold of Brie's arms, holding onto them. So, that she couldn't swing.

"What the fuck is wrong wit'chu?" I yelled. My face felt like it was on fire from being slapped several times.

"What's wrong with me?" She shrieked, her chest heaving up and down rapidly with each breath that she took.

"Yeah, what the fuck is wrong wit'chu? You flippin out putting your hands on me and shit. All because Yaya was at the same fuckin spot as us. How the fuck is that my fault?"

"Nigga don't try and flip this shit. I slapped you because of what you just said not because she was at the restaurant!" She clarified. "How do you think you sound, talking about, you didn't want to see her with another nigga? You really gone sit here and say that shit to my face and not expect me to feel some kind of way? Really?"

"I didn't want to see her ass at all!" I roared, yelling in her face. Droplets of saliva shot from my mouth, landing on her face. It wasn't intentional but in this moment I didn't even care about spitting on her. The way she'd just put her hands on me, made me want to intentionally spit on her. One of my pet peeves was someone putting their hands on me. I didn't care who it was. I didn't play that shit. Brie was definitely lucky I wasn't the type of man to put my hands on a woman.

The car fell silent, and we both sat wearing evil scowls and glaring at each other. I still had a firm grip on her arms. I didn't trust letting her go ijust yet. The look in her eyes told me the second I let go of her, she was going to try something stupid, and I didn't know how much more of her physical assault I could take before retaliating. Honestly, I was beyond fed up with this shit and in this moment, the reason I'd chosen to try and make our relationship work didn't even seem worth it. I just wanted to be done with Brie's mentally unstable ass.

"Let go of my arms. You're hurting me." Brie's voice broke the silence, as she attempted to wriggle her arms free of my grip.

I loosened my grip enough to give her some relief but not enough so that she could break free.

"Let go of my fuckin arms!" Brie shouted again, still trying to snatch away. "Why the fuck are you holding my arms?"

"You know why the fuck I'm holding your arms. Because if you swing and hit me again, I'm going to beat your ass. So, to avoid that and the consequences that comes with it, I'm going to continue holding your arms until you calm down." I explained.

"I'm calm. Now let me go." She sucked her teeth.

"Brie listen, I'm really not playing with you. If I let go of you and you put your hands on me. I'm going to beat your ass on side of this road. So you need to decide whether your arms being free is a good idea."

She jerked her arms, again. "Let go!"

This time, I let go. "Brie, I'm not playing with you." I warned.

"And I ain't playing, either!" She spat rubbing her arms where I had been holding her. "You hurt my fuckin arms. You that upset because that hoe out with someone else?"

Sometimes I wondered if she even thought before speaking because if she did, it didn't show. Here she was accusing me of holding her because of me being upset about Yaya being out with Dro. It's like she totally disregarded the fact that she'd just being slapping and punching me. Instead of responding, I put the car in drive and pulled back onto the highway. Thankfully, Brie took heed to my warning and sat in her seat and acted with some sense. I did over the speed limit all the way home. I didn't even care about getting stopped. I'd rather pay a speeding ticket than to be stuck in the car with her any longer than I had to be.

When we arrived at home, Brie jumped out the car and slammed the door. I waited till she got inside the apartment before putting the car in reverse and leaving. I knew if I went inside the two of us would end up arguing for hours or all night because once she got started, she didn't know when to stop. Also, I knew that things would turn physical. I wasn't trying to go there with her because I definitely planned on hitting her ass back this time. So to avoid all of that I left. Not just because of that. I needed to see Yaya and find out what the hell was going on with her and Dro.

Yaya

After sitting at the bar having a few more drinks with Dro, he insisted on following me home to make sure I got there safely. I was a bit hesitant at first because I didn't want him getting any ideas. I'd meant what I'd said about not crossing any inappropriate lines with him because of Keema. However, I was flattered that he cared about my safety. So, I didn't decline his offer. It was actually refreshing to see a guy behaving like a gentleman because this day in time it's rare.

On the drive from Franklin to Boykins, I kept glancing in the mirror, blushing each time I saw Dro's headlights. Him insisting on following me made me feel special. It made me feel important to someone and I liked how it felt. It didn't hurt that he'd kept me laughing and had kept my mind off of Choc for the past few hours. I was definitely glad that I'd decided to go out and glad that I'd bumped into Dro. In talking to him, I learned quite a few things about him. He seemed to be a very down to earth guy. Mostly laidback and stayed out of the way. His focus was making money and providing a better life for his son than he'd had. I respected that a lot. I also learned that we had a few things in common, like our love for live music and arcades. I could definitely see the two of us becoming good friends and I wasn't against that at all. I just wasn't sure how Keema might feel about that, and I didn't want any unnecessary over a man. I'd had my share of tussling with a bitch about her baby daddy. Lord knows, Brie and I had had our moments over Choc when she'd first found out about me because she was the picking type. She lived for drama and bullshit. Which is why I now had her blocked on every social media platform. I just wanted to live, heal, and be drama free.

Arriving at my driveway, I realized that a drama free life was not in the cards for me tonight. Choc's car was parked in my driveway, and he was leaning against it smoking a cigarette. *Choc? What the fuck is he doing here?* I froze stomping the breaks. I momentarily debated whether or not I should turn in the driveway or keep going. The honking of Dro's horn behind me caused me to ease up off the brake and turn into the driveway slowly. My heart was racing, and I wasn't sure of what to expect. I parked my car next to Choc's and got out. By now he was walking to the car and Dro had pulled into the driveway behind me. *Fuck! He sees I'm safe! Why in the fuck didn't he keep going?*

"So, this is what the fuck you got going on? You fuckin this nigga?" Choc roared as he approached me, tossing his cigarette onto the lawn.

"Choc why are you here?" I questioned, nervous and irritated by his behavior.

"Fuck all that why I'm here shit! Why the fuck is this nigga here?" He wanted to know. "I ain't been gone but a month and you're already fuckin this nigga? I should've known you were just like the rest of these bitches out here. Trying to act like you're so different."

"Hold on! Who the fuck are you calling a bitch?" I closed the small gap between us and yelled up at him, as he towered over me like a 6ft giant.

"Y'all chill!" Dro interjected walking towards Choc and I but stopping a few feet away. I assumed so that Choc wouldn't feel threatened and swing. That was a smart move because Choc would definitely blank if he felt like Dro was walking up on him to do something.

"You shut the fuck up, nigga! Don't address me. This is between me and my girl. You can get the fuck on cause ain't shit here for you, bro!" Choc let Dro know taking a few steps in Dro's direction.

I reached out quickly and grabbed the back of Choc's shirt. "Choc stop!"

Knocking my hand away, Choc yelled. "Keep your hands off of me!"

"Well then, chill the hell out. You're out here acting a fool for nothing! We aren't together. So why are you here acting like this?"

"You fuckin this nigga?" He wanted to know.

"No! We are just friends. Now, leave!"

"You got me fucked up. I ain't going nowhere. Tell your motherfuckin friend to leave."

"Choc…"

"Yaya, I'm about to be out. This ain't my type of scene. I don't do drama. I just wanted to make sure you got home safely." Dro announced. "You good?"

"Yeah, I'm good. Thanks for everything." I replied, feeling embarrassed.

"Yeah, she good." Choc barked, sizing Dro up.

"We'll see each other another time." Dro repeated, already heading in the direction of his car.

"We see each other, now." Choc called after him.

"Yeah, we do but I actually have respect for Iyanna. Like I said, we'll see each other another time." With that Dro got in his car and left.

"I'm definitely gonna see that nigga." Choc nodded, still looking in the direction where Dro had just been.

I felt so embarrassed. I hated that Dro had witnessed this nonsense. I looked up at Choc and anger overtook me. "Why? Why the fuck are you here? Didn't you choose your family. So why in the fuck you not with them?"

"Don't that nigga got a baby with your home girl? So, what the fuck you doing on date with him?" Choc questioned, totally disregarding everything I'd just said.

"I wasn't on no date with him. I was out by myself, having a drink, and he showed up. That's it. Stop assuming shit!"

"I saw you and that nigga eating and smiling up in each other's faces. Sure as fuck looked like a date to me."

"Wait…what? You saw me out and then came here and waited for me?" I looked at him in disbelief, shaking my head. After all this man had put me through, he had the audacity to show up to my house to question me about me being out with someone else.

"Yeah, I did because I wanted to know what was up."

"Why? You made your choice. Now stand on that. You don't have the right to come here asking me shit. If you were so concerned about me, you would've done right by me and this wouldn't even be a conversation. The fact that you feel like it's ok to do you and try to run my life at the same time, tells me you have a lot of fuckin nerve." I was done talking. The way I was feeling right now. I was subject to slap fire from him. So, I knew it was best that I walk away. I started towards the house. "You can leave."

Choc reached out and grabbed my arm pulling me back. "So, it's like that?"

"Like what?" I snapped, snatching my arm away and looking at him in disgust. "What do you want from me? You did me wrong and yet here you are demanding an explanation from me. Man, get the fuck out of my yard. You men kill me. A bitch can give y'all everything and you won't appreciate it. Y'all will drag a bitch till we don't even recognize ourselves, anymore. Meanwhile, we still fight to love you, when you're killing us emotionally. We still fight to see the good in you. None of that's enough but the moment we leave y'all the fuck alone. Here comes the fake love and concern. Where the fuck was this energy when I was investing my time and energy into you, being all about you for the past three and a half years?" I didn't wait for an answer because there really wasn't one that he could give that would even matter. "Then you come here and give me fuckin excuses after breaking my heart into pieces. Fuck your reason for choosing Brie over me. The reason doesn't matter. The bottom line is you choose her. So, stop harassing me! If you aren't happy with your decision. That's your problem not mine. Go live your life and allow me to heal and put back together what you broke." With that, I walked away.

"Ya! Ya!" Choc called after me.

I stopped for a second and looked back. "Go home to your family." I said and then walked up the steps, unlocked my door and went inside.

Inside, I tossed my things onto the sofa, flopped down next to them, and began taking off my sandals. I heard my phone vibrating in my purse. I reached over and took it out, seeing that I had a text from Choc. *Why in the fuck won't he just leave me alone?*

Choc: *Can you please come back outside. So, we can talk. I love you, for real.*

Me: *Go home and don't come back. After this text, I will be blocking you. I'm choosing myself motherfucka. I'm sure you understand.*

Soon as the message said *delivered*, I blocked Choc. I can't lie, though. I had mixed emotions about it. As angry as I was at him, I was simply trying to put on a brave front because he still had my heart in a vise grip. However, I wanted him to feel how I had felt with no way to contact me. I doubted that he would feel exactly how I'd felt but if he only felt a fraction of how I'd felt. That would be good enough for me.

I got up from the sofa and went into the kitchen. In the kitchen, I grabbed a bottle of Moscato from my wine rack and opened it. I didn't bother getting a glass. I turned the bottle up to my head and took a long swig. I needed something to calm my nerves and numb the pain. I was so sick of feeling this way. Why was I the one who had to suffer just for loving a mothafucka? Why was I being punished for having genuine love and intentions for someone? This love shit made absolutely no sense to me.

The ringing of the doorbell coupled with banging on the front door, caused me to jump. "Yaya! Open the fuckin door!" I could hear Choc yelling.

Bottle in hand, I damn near ran back through the house to the door. "Choc, stop causing a damn scene and leave! Before my neighbors call the police. Damn, just leave me alone!" I yelled through the door.

The banging stopped. Then, I heard Choc ask. "So, this nigga really got you treating me like this? You can't open the door so we can talk?"

"This has nothing to do with Dro. This is the mess you made. I'm just cleaning it up." I paused, letting out a frustrated sigh. "Choc, I'm tired. Just let it go…please."

A few seconds passed and then he said. "I love you, Ya. That ain't no lie. I've lied and fucked up countless times and I know you don't believe shit I say but that's the truth."

"Honestly, I don't think you know what love is. You take care of and protect who you love. You don't hurt, manipulate, and make a fool of them. That's not love." I replied.

"I do love you. Just open the door."

"No! Now, leave!"

"Aight, fuck it! Since you can tell me how I fuckin feel. Fuck you and that whack ass nigga."

I didn't respond. I heard him walking off the porch and then his car door slam. I walked back over to the sofa and sat down. I grabbed my cell and FaceTimed Ajah and Mari. Ajah was the first to accept.

"What's up, chick? Did you enjoy yourself? I see, you didn't find a man." She laughed.

"Girrrrl, when I tell you about the freakin night I had." I paused, taking another swig from the wine bottle. "Every other week this man is finding a new way to add to the misery he's already inflicted upon me and a new way to make me look even dumber than I already feel. My life has become a fuckin season of Love and Hip Hop!"

Ajah sat up in her recliner and muted her tv. "Hold on bitch! We gotta find out why Mari ain't picking up because…"

Before she could finish her sentence, Mari joined the FaceTime. "Hey heffas! My bad. As you can see, I'm cooking." She turned the camera. So, we could see the pots and pans on the stove. "I'm whipping up some…"

"Girl, fuck that food! Your sister about to spill some tea!" Ajah cut Mari off.

Mari flipped her camera back around to face her. "What happened?" Her eyes were big with excitement.

"Ugggh." I turned the wine bottle back up to my head and took a huge gulp. I was now wishing I hadn't called them. The look of excitement on their faces to hear about my misery was kind of offensive. Not one ounce of concern showed in either of their expressions.

"Ugggh?" Ajah questioned, a confused expression on her face. "What the hell does that mean? Tell us what happened that got you over there acting like Ned the Wino?"

"Choc happened! I'm just so sick of this never-ending toxic bullshit with him! Why won't he just leave me alone? He made his choice! So, what in the fuck does he want from me? Why can't he just let me heal and get past this? Why keep fuckin with me?" I exploded and so did my tear ducts. Tears rolled down my cheeks. Emotionally, I was exhausted. "I hate I ever met that man. I swear!"

"Ummm…not trying to be funny or insensitive but we still don't know what happened because you're sorta speaking in riddles." Mari replied.

I wiped my tears with the back of my hand and began to explain what had happened. "I went to El Rancheros to get out of the house. I was at the bar and Keema's baby daddy came in. So, we had a few drinks and chopped it up. When we were done, he insisted on following me home to make sure I got here safely. When we got here. Choc was here. He started going off, asking me was I fuckin Dro. He wanted to fight Dro because he was trying to defuse the situation. Apparently, Choc was at El Rancheros and saw us and that's what set him off." I shook my head. "Then after Dro left and I came inside. He's outside at the door banging on the door and ringing the doorbell, acting a damn fool."

Mari and Ajah both erupted with laughter.

"That's what his ass get!" Mari laughed, while clapping her hands. "Made that damn chest hurt seeing you with somebody else. Tell him don't cry at the door like a little bitch! Take that shit like you did!"

"I know that's right!" Ajah chimed in. "Ain't no fun when the rabbit got the gun." She laughed.

"You're better than me because when he asked if I was fuckin Dro, I would've said yes!" Mari commented.

"Me too girl!" Ajah agreed.

"But I'm not though and I don't want it getting out that I am because then I'll have to deal with Keema and I ain't about to be arguing over no man. Especially one that I ain't dealing with." I told them.

"Keema had better sit her ass down somewhere if she knows what's good for her. She don't want no smoke. She doesn't own that man. She can't say nothing with how she be bussin it open for everybody." Ajah replied.

"That part!" Mari said and then left the camera to go tend to her food.

"Nah, I ain't trying to have no issues with her. I wouldn't want my friend messing with my baby daddy." I admitted. "So, I wouldn't do that to anyone else."

"Girl, you have really gotta stop acting like you're Mother Teresa and live. Keema wouldn't care about you if the shoe was on the other foot." Ajah wouldn't let up. "Tell me this. Did you enjoy yourself with Dro?"

"Yeah, I did." I blushed just thinking of how much I'd enjoyed Dro's company. I'd actually had a great time until I got home. It'd been a while since I'd laughed so much.

"See, look at you blushing." Mari was back at the camera. "No one is telling you to marry him or sleep with him…"

"I did!" Ajah yelled.

"Anyways…" Mari continued. "Just enjoy yourself. You can have friends and hang out. You don't owe Choc an explanation for shit. He made his choice."

"That's true." I agreed, before putting the wine bottle to my lips and downing the rest of its contents.

"On another note, you need to stop drinking and take your tipsy ass to bed." Ajah told me.

"I'm going." I said, feeling the effects of the bottle of wine I'd just downed.

"And don't go texting or calling Choc because you're drunk. Let that nigga stay where he is." Mari added. "Remember you don't owe him shit. And on some real shit I'm proud of you for not folding for him like you normally do. Make him stand on his shit. He chose his baby mama, let him stay over there with her. You ain't nobody's second choice."

"Thanks, sis." I replied. "Well, good night y'all."

"Good night." They both replied in unison.

I hung up and then opened my Messenger app and went to Dro's name.

Me: Hey. I just wanted to apologize for how Choc acted tonight. I had no idea he would be here or do anything like that. I'm really sorry.

After sending the message, I got up and took my empty wine bottle into the kitchen and tossed it in the trash. Leaving out of the kitchen, I turned off all the lights throughout the front of the house and made sure the front door was locked. When I was done, I grabbed my phone off the coffee table and went down the hall to my bedroom. The wine I'd drank had me tipsy as hell. Not bothering to undress, I laid across the end of my bed and checked my phone. I saw that Dro had messaged me back.

Dro: You don't have to apologize for that insecure nigga. We good, baby. All he did was make me want you more. If you got a nigga sitting outside your house, waiting on you, ready to lose his life behind you. You definitely gotta be some pressure. Which I already knew that, anyways. He knows that he done fucked up. Just so you know, idgaf about Keema. I'm on your ass. GN beautiful.

Instead of responding, I just got off my phone completely. I was speechless. I couldn't believe what I'd just read and I wasn't sure of how to feel about it. It was something about the arrogant way he responded, not in a bad way but in a way that made me feel things I shouldn't. Things like, my coochie becoming moist. Maybe it was just finally having someone pursue me or show me some attention that had me feeling some type of way. Whatever it was. I knew it was best I didn't respond.

Dro

"Man, you should've seen how that nigga was spazzing like he was really about to do something to me. Cuz, I'm telling you. He'd better be glad I've changed because if he had caught me back in the day and tried that shit. I would've left that nigga laying in that driveway." I told Tre. It was Sunday afternoon, and he was cutting my hair at his crib. He had a shed in his back yard where he cut hair on the weekends.

"Wait so, you fuckin Choc's girl?" Tre laughed. "Nigga take it from me, leave that shit alone. If she's his bitch, let him have her. Don't start going back and forth with that nigga fighting over no pussy. You see all the shit I went through all over some pussy."

"First off, I ain't fuckin Iyanna and she ain't no bitch. I bumped into her at El Rancheros. We had a few drinks, some food, and then I followed her home to make sure she got there safely. That was it. That insecure nigga was in his feelings, jumping to conclusions. She's not his woman. He's just salty because he left her, and he knows a real one bout to snatch her fine ass up." I let him know. Then added. "And you didn't go through all the shit you went through bout no pussy. Nigga, you fell in love with

172

Lala and couldn't leave her alone. It was about more than the pussy. That woman had left Boykins and you still couldn't stay away. That definitely wasn't just about no pussy. If I recall correctly, you and her were kickin it pretty hard before she got pregnant. So, tell that shit to somebody who doesn't know any better."

When Tre responded, his tone had changed. "Yeah, you're right. It was definitely about more than pussy."

"Hold up, nigga. Do you need a second to get yourself together? You ain't bout to be crying while you're cutting my hair and fuck my shit up." I laughed, trying to lighten the mood.

"Yeah, you're right. Give me a second." Tre replied, turning off the clippers.

I looked back at him and saw the sadness in his eyes. The pain in his eyes was heartbreaking. *And this nigga talking about, he went through hell over some pussy. He went through hell for love.* I didn't speak my thoughts, but it was clear to see that after all this time, Tre still loved Lala and missed her dearly. His love for her was the type of love I craved to have with someone.

"You good man? I didn't mean to bring up…"

"I'm good man. You ain't did nothing wrong." He held up his hand, cutting me off. He took a seat, grabbed his pack of Newports from the counter, and shook one from the pack. After lighting his cigarette, he took a drag. Looking off across the room, as if he was deep in thought. He shook his head. I could see water glistening in his eyes. "It's just still hard to talk about her. I regret so much shit, man. I wish like hell that life had a reset button. I'd do so many things differently. She deserved so much better than what she got." He paused and shook his head, again. "Then, there's Kisha. What kind of a mother would purposely harm her children and just leave them? Sometimes, I sit, and wonder does she even think about them or regret what she did."

"So, there's still no word on where she is?" I questioned.

"Hell, nah." Tre replied, wiping his eyes with the back of his hand. "At first, a part of me felt sorry for her and I didn't want her to get caught. I was just grateful that my boys were alive but now. Every morning, I wake up. I pray they catch her ass and put her under the jail. My boys struggle every day to cope with their injuries and just be normal kids. She took a lot from them. All to get back at me and for what really? She was fuckin Skeet the whole time I was fuckin Lala. So, what was the point of harming my kids? Not just my kids but the kids that she carried inside of her for nine months. I just don't get it."

I shook my head this time. "I agree. That was some fucked up shit she did. You're a better man than me, cuz. I would be hunting her ass down myself."

"Nah. My kids need me. I'm all they have left. My girls no longer have a mother because of me. So, I owe it to them and my boys to be the best father I can be. That's why I work and bring my ass home. I rarely even go to Lizzie's like I used to. I can't afford to be out there like I used to because if I fuck up, everything will be left on my mom. My dad's gone. So, it's just me and her. She's getting older. She can't handle all the responsibility that comes with taking care of four children. Two of which is disabled."

"Yeah, that is a lot."

"Yeah, that's why I'm going to let God handle Kisha."

"I hear you and you're absolutely right, but I'd still have to find Kisha and fuck her up!" I laughed but I was as serious as a heart attack.

Tre erupted with laughter. "Boy, I swear you remind me of how I used to be. The old Tre would've sent her ass to meet Jesus. You know how I used to get down."

"Hell, yeah! Boy, you're a legend in this here small town." I acknowledged.

"For all the wrong reasons." He replied, putting his cigarette out and grabbing the clippers. He walked back over and began cutting my hair, again.

While he cut my hair, I took out my phone and texted Keema.

Me: Hey. If you aren't busy, I'd like to come by and get lil man for a little while.

Keema: He's not with me. My home girl, Yaya has him. Where you picked him up from before.

Me: Why does she have him?

Keema: Because I had plans and I needed someone to watch him.

Me: Why didn't you just call me?

Keema: Dro just go get him from Yaya. I don't feel like going back and forth. I'll let her know you're coming to get him.

Me: I'm getting my hair cut right. Let her know I'll be there in about forty-five minutes.

Keema: Ok.

"So, back to Yaya. What's the real deal? I can tell you're really diggin her but why her? I mean, you know, dealing with her will stir up a bunch of drama. So, why even go down that road?" Tre inquired.

I slipped my phone back in my pocket and took a few seconds to gather my thoughts. I didn't want to speak too fast and not articulate myself correctly. "She's different. Yeah, she's beautiful but it's deeper than that. She's intelligent, has a successful career, open-minded, funny, and just all-around dope. Unfortunately, we both have people from our past that would hate seeing us together but fuck'em. I look at it like this, my relationship with Keema didn't work out for whatever reason and neither did her situation with ol boy. That's our past. If we hit it off and make each other happy. That's all that matters. I'll never let my past dictate my future."

"I hear all of that and you're going to do what you want regardless but I just want you to really sit down and consider if this woman is really worth the headache." Tre cautioned. "I don't know Choc that well and I don't know to what extent he'll go to, to hold on to this woman but apparently, he doesn't plan on giving up without a fight."

I waved him off dismissively. "Man, fuck Choc. I ain't worried about that nigga. Like I said before, fuck him, Keema, and anyone else who feels some type of way about me talking to Iyanna. I'm a grown ass man and that's the bottom line."

"Okay, cuz. I hear ya." Tre replied, removing the barber cape from around me.

I stood up and looked in the mirror. "You always get me right, cuz." I told him, nodding my approval. I reached in my pocket, took out my wallet, and paid him. "Thanks man. I'm gonna bring DJ by here next weekend. So, you can get him right for me."

"Alright, that'll work."

"If you ain't doing nothing later, I might come back through and have a few drinks with you. I have a bottle of Patron in my truck." I said, as I made my way to the door.

"Shit, you need to give me a drink of that right now." Tre said, lighting another cigarette, while heading towards the door. "Let me go grab a cup."

"Nigga, I ain't say you could have a drink of my shit now. I ain't even opened it yet."

"Shit, now or later, what's the difference?" He wanted to know. "Besides, I'm still big cuz. I'll take that shit!" He said running up behind me and playfully grabbing me in a headlock. "Yeah, talk that shit now lil nigga."

I elbowed him in the stomach, and we fell to the ground, rolling around like two children. In the past few years, we'd grown close since Keema moved back to Boykins and I was around more. He'd helped me through some tough times, and I'd done the same for him. This was my nigga for life. The fact that we were blood only made our bond tighter but I honestly because if we'd just randomly met each other, we'd still be close. Tre was a real nigga. Life and unfortunate circumstances had changed him a lot. Not in a bad way but it had made him more cautious of the choices he made. He realized now that every action had a reaction. So, he moved a lot differently than before. Which was good because times where I wanted to wild out and make decisions based off emotions. He would be right there to bring me back to reality and remind me of all that I had to lose and of how far I'd come. I appreciated him for that. Don't get it twisted. I was still my own man and the final decision on whether to do some crazy shit or not do it was all mine, but I did value his opinion and his wisdom.

"If y'all don't get y'all black asses up off that ground, rolling around like two fools!" Aunt Dorothy laughed, standing over us with her hand on her hip. "Come help me get the boys out of the car."

Tre and I got off the ground, brushing grass from our clothes.

"Ma, where's Laila and Lola." Tre wanted to know.

"Chile, we saw their other grandma in Walmart, and they left my tail. She said if you want her to bring them back later, she will but if not, they can stay the night."

"Say less." Tre replied, heading towards her minivan to get the boys. I was right behind him. "She can keep them two worrisome thangs tomorrow night, too."

"Yeah, right. You say that now and will be calling asking her to bring them home as soon as you open your eyes in the morning." Aunt Dorothy replied.

"He ain't that bad is he, auntie?" I laughed.

"Boy, he can't stand for any of these kids to be out of his sight for too long. He talks that mess, but those kids keep him going."

"Aye, ain't nothing wrong with that. I'm about to go get my lil man when I leave here."

"I know, Keema probably standing outside waiting on your ass." Tre teased, as he lifted Quan out of the car while I assisted Shaun.

"Nah, he's at Yaya's crib." I informed him.

He stopped walking and looked back at me. Instead of saying anything, he just laughed, shook his head, and then continued inside the house.

"What?"

"I don't have anything to say."

"Yeah, you do nigga. Say it."

"Be careful. That's all I'm going to say." He warned.

"Man, I'm just going to pick up DJ. That's all." I assured him.

"Yeah…okay." He replied, sarcastically.

"Whatever man."

After getting the boys situated, I gave Tre a drink and then headed to Iyanna's house to pick up DJ.

****

When I arrived, Iyanna opened the door wearing a long yellow skirt with the tube top to match. The yellow against her chocolate complexion caused my manhood to rise. I prayed she didn't notice. My eyes traveled down to the colorful waist beads around her waist. *This woman is so fuckin sexy, effortlessly.*

"Hey. Come on in." She smiled, holding the door open for me. Her voice was different, she sounded stuffy.

"Hey." I replied, walking inside. There were candles and incenses lit and 90's R&B spilled from the speaker of the Alexa device sitting on the mantle. I also picked up on the smell of food in the air. "What you got going on up in here? You trying to set the mood for me or something?" I teased.

"What? No." She giggled, showing off the sexy gap between her two front teeth. I'd always had a thing for women with gaps. "I just enjoy a relaxed vibe when I'm home. So, I lit a few incenses and candles after saging the house earlier. Plus, I haven't been feeling too well today but I've been trying to stay up and moving."

Again, I was impressed by her. She was different from any woman I'd ever met, and that shit was so attractive. She had me so intrigued. I wanted to know everything about her. The fact that she wasn't feeling well and was still willing to care for my son made me want to care for her. I don't care what she said. I was determined to have her.

"DJ's down the hall in my room taking a nap. I can go and wake him if you want, or you can chill for a minute until he wakes up. It's up to you." Iyanna announced. "He's got a little cold. So, he was a little cranky before he fell asleep. Honestly, I think I caught his cold."

"A cold? How long has he been here?" I asked, this was my first-time hearing anything about him being sick. Keema hadn't mentioned anything.

"Since like ten this morning."

"Ten this morning?" I repeated, wondering what was so important that Keema had dropped DJ off at ten in the morning and here it was past three in the afternoon.

"Yeah, Keema said she was going with Hakeem to Richmond for the day. They'd made plans earlier in the week and she didn't have a sitter. I wasn't doing anything. So, I didn't mind." She said, taking a seat on the sofa. "Have a seat."

"Nah, I'm gonna just take DJ and go. So, that you can get some rest. I apologize for you having to watch him when you're not feeling well. I had no idea he was here until like an hour ago. Keema knows that she could've called me." I told her. It annoyed me that not only had Keema dropped him off to go run behind a man but to drop him when he wasn't feeling well was just triflin.

"I...ha-chew!" Iyanna sneezed and then made a sniffling noise.

"Bless you."

"Thanks. I knew I was going to catch DJ's cold when he was over here the other day. Keema said he'd been coughing since they went to the pool last weekend."

"Have you taken anything?"

"Nah, I was going to run out, but DJ was so fussy. I didn't want to take him out."

"What do you take?"

"Mucinex."

"I'll run to the store, real quick, and get you something. Do you know if DJ has taken anything?"

"Yeah, Keema has been giving him cough syrup. It's in his bag. I gave him some before he went to sleep."

"Okay, well, I'll just grab something for you." I told her, already headed for the door.

"Wait let me grab my purse." She said jumping up from the sofa.

"Iyanna if you don't sit down. You don't ever need your purse around me." I winked at her and then turned and left before she could refuse.

At the store, I grabbed Mucinex, a few cans of chicken noodle soup, juice, and some snacks for DJ. When I got back, Iyanna had just finished cooking. She offered me a plate.

"Yeah, let me see if you can throw down in the kitchen." I teased, while leaning against the counter, watching her fix both our plates. She'd prepared baked salmon, asparagus, garlic mashed potatoes, macaroni and cheese, and dinner rolls.

"Boy, bye. I be…" She started coughing and hurriedly put down the plate she was fixing and covered her mouth.

I picked up the plate from the counter. "Go take some of those Mucinex tablets and drink some juice. I got this.

"You sure? You don't even know where everything is." She hesitated. Her eyes were now watery, and her voice cracked.

"Woman this kitchen ain't but so big. I'm sure I will find everything just fine but if I can't. I can always ask you. Now, go take something for that cold. I don't need you giving me your cooties, making me sick."

"Thanks for helping. I apologize. You're a guest, you shouldn't be in here fixing plates."

"I'm also a man and I would be less than that if I sat here and see you sick and not help. Especially, when you've been taking care of my sick child all day. While not feeling well yourself. I don't know what type of man you think I am, but I look out for and take care of any woman in my presence. Especially one that I want." I let her know. "Now, go in the living room and sit down. I'll bring your plate to you."

"I'm not even going to entertain that slick comment about you wanting me. I told you already that isn't going to happen." She blushed.

"Yeah ok. That look on your face is saying something different."

"I'm going in the living room." She said, sucking her teeth.

"That's what you were told to do, anyways."

"You're DJ's daddy not mine sir."

"I'm about to be yours, too." I laughed.

She laughed, too. "Bye Dro. I'm going in the living room." She started out of the kitchen. I watched as she walked out and noticed the extra switch in her wide hips.

"Daddy will be in there in a minute, baby." I called after her.

"Shut up, Dro." She yelled back.

I just laughed and continued fixing our plates. When I was done, I took our plates in the living room. After handing her to her, I sat down on the other end of the sofa with mine.

"You saying grace or me?" I asked.

A confused expression covered her face. "Grace?"

"Yeah, grace. You don't bless your food before eating?" I looked at her with raised eyebrows.

She shook her head. "Nah, I ain't even gone sit here and lie to you. I just sit down and eat."

"Oh, we gotta change that. I thank God for every meal. That's just how I was raised." I told her.

"Okay. Well, you go on and say grace. Next time, I'll do it."

I looked at her and smiled.

"What?"

"Nothing." I replied, before bowing my head and blessing the food.

Choc

A month later...

I woke up to an empty bed. I was kind of glad because it gave me a few minutes to get my head together before having to get up and get dressed for work. As I laid there looking up at the ceiling, my mind went to the one place it had been for the past month...Yaya. I'd called and texted numerous times and gotten no reply. I'd unblocked her on Facebook and sent her a friend request. She never accepted. I'd gone by her house. Only for her to ignore me or yell through the door and ask me to leave. She was treating me as if I was a complete stranger. I ain't no bitch or simp ass nigga but that shit was getting to me bad. The thing that was really killing me was, a few times I'd driven past her house and seen Dro's car in the driveway. She'd lied to me and told me; she wasn't fuckin with this nigga. It killed me to think about him touching her and to think about her doing all the things for the next nigga that she'd done for me. I knew the kind of woman Yaya was and I knew that if Dro had his hooks in her he wasn't letting go because she was a damn good woman. I felt like the biggest fool for choosing Brie over her. I'd lost a good woman all because I couldn't let go of my past. Now, here I was miserable and stuck with Brie, who was on my last nerve. If I'm being honest, it wasn't even anything that she was doing to irritate me. Sure, she was still being Brie, but I was used to that. I was angry at her because she wasn't Yaya. That wasn't her fault. It was mine. I should've chosen Yaya and gotten custody of my kids like I'd thought about doing so many times before making my decision. The damage was done now but I wasn't giving up easily. Yaya may have been fuckin with Dro but I knew without a doubt she still loved me, and that no nigga could replace me. Dro was simply a rebound. She was doing that shit out of hurt. Probably to get back at me for choosing Brie. I understood it but if she thought I was gonna sit back while she moved on with the next nigga. She was in for a rude awakening. Yaya was mine and nothing was gonna change that.

"Da, where's Jada?" Justice asked, as he approached the bed, rubbing sleep from his eyes.

I'd been so caught up with my thoughts of Yaya that I hadn't heard him come in. I turned to look at him. "They are probably in the living room. Go in there and look." I told him.

"They aren't in there and they left the door opened." He informed me. "Ma said we ain't supposed to leave the door open because bad people might come in."

I sat up, tossing the covers back. "What'chu mean the door is open?" I was already heading out of the bedroom to go and see what in the hell was going on. Sure enough, when I walked in the living room, the front door was open. "What in the fuck?" I mumbled. I closed the door, then went back down the hall to the bedroom, and grabbed my cell. I went to Brie's name and pressed it. The phone didn't even ring it went straight to voicemail. I tried, again. The same thing happened. Justice was standing in the doorway. "Go put your shoes on." I told him and then began grabbing clothes from the drawer, throwing them on. I grabbed my kids and cell. Justice met me in the hallway. "Come on. We gotta go find your mom and sister." I said, already heading towards the front door. I had a bad feeling about this. The first thing that popped in my head was Brie was back fucking with drugs. That had to be it. Where else was she in such a rush to get to so early in the morning that she'd left the door open and not woken me up.

When we got to the car, I called Brie's mom. She answered on the second ring.

"Hey Choc." She answered, dryly.

"Hey, Donna. Have you seen Brie? She left before I woke up and took Jada with her, but the front door was left open." I explained, turning out of our apartment complex, with no real destination.

"Naw, I haven't. Where on earth do you think she went this early in the morning? She ain't back on that stuff, is she? I ain't playing about…"

"Fuck!" I yelled, cutting her off and coming to a stop because the road was blocked off by police and an ambulance. "Donna let me call you back." I said hanging up before she could respond. I unbuckled my seatbelt. So, I could get out and get a closer look at what was going on. Before getting out, I looked back at Justice and said. "Stay here. I'll be right back."

"Where you going?" He asked, trying to unbuckle his seatbelt.

"Just do what I said." I snapped and then hurried up the street. There were several people out of their cars trying to get a better look at what was going on as well. I pushed my way through the crowd. I could see something lying in the street covered by a sheet.

As I was passing by two women, one said. "Poor baby. It doesn't make any sense how irresponsible these parents are. I hope they lock their asses up."

The other woman replied. "Me too!"

I stopped and asked. "What happened?" My voice was trembling.

"A little girl got hit by a truck. The guy that hit her said she just walked out in front of him, and he couldn't stop."

I started pushing everyone out of my way, trying to get to the sheet in the street. "Move! Move the fuck out of the way!" I yelled, fighting my way through the crowd.

"Hey man, watch where the fuck you're going!" A heavy-set white guy yelled, pushing me back.

I pushed him, again. So hard that he stumbled, bumping into the people next to him. "Move the fuck out my way!" I didn't wait for any retaliation because I didn't have time. I needed to see if that was my baby lying in the street.

Two officers met me just as I made my way to the front of the crowd. "Sir, you need to stay back."

"I need to see if that's my daughter. Her and her mother were gone when I got up and the door was left open!" I screamed.

The officers looked at each other and then the older white cop told me to come with them. They walked me over to the sheet and lifted it a little. I fell to my knees next to my baby, laying there lifeless on the ground. "God nooooooo!" I wailed.

"Sir, we need you to come with us. We need to ask you a few questions." The older officer told me, grabbing my arm and trying to pull me up, while the other officer covered Jada back up.

"No, I'm not leaving her!" I fought against him.

"Sir, you have to." He told me.

The other officer yelled over to the paramedics and told them to come get Jada off the ground.

"No! Don't touch her! Get the fuck away from her!" I fought. More officers came over and assisted with dragging me off the ground and away from Jada's body as the paramedics worked fast to get her off the ground and into the ambulance. I felt so helpless. How the fuck had this happened?

Once the officers got me over to their cruiser, they forced me inside.

"I need to get my son!" I told the officers.

"Where's your son, sir?" The older officer asked.

"He's in my car. We stopped to see what was going on. I told him to wait for me till I got back."

"Okay what kind of car do you have?" He wanted to know.

"It's a charcoal gray 2018 Infinity." I told him.

"I'll go and get your son." He promised.

"What about my car?"

"Give me your keys, sir."

I fished my keys out of my pocket and handed them to him. He took them and walked off.

"Okay sir, I'm Officer Williams." The young black officer formally introduced himself. "And your name is?"

My head felt like it was spinning. I couldn't think straight or focus on what he was saying because images of Jada's lifeless body were flooding my head. Holding my head in my hands, I broke down, weeping like a child. "How the fuck did this happen? How did she get out of the house?" I cried and then out of nowhere, rage consumed me. "Brie had to have left the door open. She had to! I swear to God when I lay eyes on that bitch!" I hit the dashboard of the cruiser. "Y'all may as well get ready to lock my black ass up!"

"Calm down, sir." Officer Williams spoke calmly. "I understand that you are upset but I can't allow you to make threats on someone's life."

"Threats?" I questioned, looking at him through tear filled eyes. "My…baby is…gone." My voice cracked, saying that made my chest physically hurt. "I'm not…m-making threats. It's a promise."

"Sir, tell me your name."

"Justin Branch." I ran my hand down my face to wipe the tears away. My eyes went over to the spot where Jada had been laying. Her body was gone now. I broke down again. "This shit ain't right. My baby didn't deserve that."

"No sir, she didn't." Officer Williams looked at me. His eyes were sympathetic. "I want to offer you my sincerest condolences. I know that doesn't help but I am truly sorry for your loss."

I didn't respond. I just looked out the window. When I did, I saw Brie walking through the crowd, looking spaced out. The spaced-out look in her eyes told me exactly where she'd been. I opened the door and jumped out. I heard Officer Williams calling after me, telling me to stop and come back but his demands fell on deaf ears. Within seconds, I'd reached Brie. I grabbed her, turned her around, and began shaking her. "Where the fuck have you been? My fuckin baby is dead because of you! You druggy bitch!"

"Jada's at the playground." Brie slurred, as her head moved back and forth like a rag doll from me shaking her.

"I left her on the playground. I told her to play until I got back."

I snapped and grabbed her by her throat. "You dumb bitch! You left my baby on the playground to go get high." I was trying to squeeze the life out of her. I wanted her to die right there in the street like Jada had.

"Let go of her!" I heard officers yelling, as they grabbed me, dragging me away from Brie.

"I'm gonna kill that bitch! Jail is too good for her!" I roared.

Brie was rubbing her neck and coughing. "What's wrong...with you? Jada's at the playground." She looked at the officers. "She's at the playground."

"Ma'am, I need for you to put your hands behind your back. You're under arrest." Officer Williams told her.

"For what? Jada's at the playground. If you would just go look. I told her to play till I got back." She was still coughing and rubbing her throat.

"Ma'am, your daughter is dead. She was hit by a truck a little over an hour ago. Due to your neglect," He didn't wait for a response. He just grabbed her arm and put one of the cuffs on. When he tried to do the other, she began resisting. So, one of the other officers assisted him. After getting the cuffs on her. They read her her rights, and then walked her over to one of the cruisers and placed her in the back.

"Sir, you are under arrest as well for assault." One of the officers told me as he began placing the cuffs on me and reading me my rights.

"Under arrest? That bitch killed my child, and you are arresting me?" I asked in disbelief.

"Sir, I understand the severity of what she did but it's still against the law to assault anyone." He told me as they all but dragged me towards the me police cruiser.

I fought until they got me inside. "I can't just leave my son! My fuckin son is still in the car."

The older white officer got in the driver's seat and looked back at me. "Sir, your son is fine. He's with one of the other officers. I'm sure they've probably called CPS."

"I don't need no fuckin CPS for my son! I can take care of him myself."

"No sir, you can't. Not where you're going." He told me. Then, he turned around, put the car in drive, and drove off.

I kicked and yelled obscenities for most of the drive but he simply ignored me. Growing tired and feeling helpless, I rested my head on the back of the seat, while tears spilled from the corners of my eyes. As fucked up as it may sound, my mind went to Yaya. *If I'd chosen Yaya none of this shit would be happening.* I blamed myself.

Dro

"You know it's really funny how you went from, I can't mess with you to me waking up in your bed." I told Iyanna as we lay in her bed talking for the second morning in a row.

"Hush, I still haven't *messed* with you." She giggled, moving her locs behind her shoulders. She looked like a goddess to me even before washing her face.

"That's because I'm a gentleman and I haven't been applying pressure on getting your goodies, but I can tell by how you look at me. You want me to open up that cookie jar."

"You really make me sick!" She laughed.

I watched as she laughed, enjoying the happiness in her face. When we'd initially started kickin it, her eyes held a sadness that broke my heart because I knew hers had been broken. I'd wanted to take her pain away and over the past few weeks I'd watched it slowly fade away. I knew she still loved Choc and I wasn't threatened by it at all. I understood it. That just made me want her more because I knew she was a woman who loved hard and fully committed herself to whomever she was involved with.

"Why are you staring at me like that?" She asked, fidgeting with one of her locs.

I removed her hand from her hair. Putting it up to my lips, I kissed the back of it. "For one because you're beautiful and secondly because I love seeing you happy."

"Thanks." She blushed. "I'm just glad to not be walking around sad and feeling like shit every day."

"Yeah, it sucks that you had to go through that but that shit only made you stronger. Now, that you've been through that. You'll never allow someone to do that to you again. Especially not him."

"I don't want to talk about that anymore." She looked at me and I saw the sadness had returned.

"My bad, beautiful. How about you get dressed? We go to NC and stop by my house. So, I can get dressed. Then we go have breakfast somewhere." I suggested.

"That sounds like a plan." She replied, as the smile returned to her lips. She tossed back the covers and got up.

I watched as she walked across the room in the black biker shorts and wife beater, she'd slept in. *Good lord, it's becoming harder to remain a gentleman.* So far, we'd only kissed but I wasn't sure of how much longer I would be able to lay next to her, cuddling her from behind without hitting her from behind. I wanted to do everything to her. Shit that I'd never done to any other woman. I don't know what it was that had me so gone over this woman but from the first night I'd come over to pick up DJ, I'd felt a connection to her. It was almost magnetic. Like something was drawing me to her and I couldn't fight it.

Grabbing her robe from the hanger on the back of the door. She looked back at me. "I won't be long."

"Take your time. I ain't going nowhere." I replied winking at her.

She blushed and left the room, and I got up and made the bed.

"Why the hell does this woman need all these pillows when she only has one damn head." I said aloud, shaking my head. "Women."

When I was done making the bed, I got dressed. I was sitting on the side of the bed, putting my shoes on, when Iyanna walked back into the room. The smell of vanilla invaded my nostrils. She smelled good enough to eat.

"Ummm, can you excuse me while I get dressed?" She smiled.

I finished tying my shoe and then got up and walked over to her. Stopping directly in front of her. "You sure you don't need any assistance?"

"Yes sir, I'm sure. Now get your butt out of here."
She pushed me playfully.

I pulled her into me, wrapping my arms around her.
Then I leaned down and covered her lips with mine. As we
kissed my hands moved down, cupping her round backside.
A soft moan escaped her throat, and I felt her hand against
my chest, slightly pushing me back. She pulled away and
looked up at me.

"Chill. We can't do this till I talk to Keema. I told
you that." She said.

"Iyanna, I don't need no permission from Keema to
do shit. I don't know why you feel like you do. That girl
ain't thinking about us. She's out here living her best life
playing hopscotch from one dick to the next." I explained.
"Not just that but we've kissed and spent countless nights
together. You've already crossed this imaginary girl code
line. So, stop playing games and act your age. I don't like
games. It's either you're fuckin with me or you're not."

She looked shocked by the things I'd just said or
maybe it had been my tone. I hadn't meant for my words to
come out so harshly, but I'd meant every word I'd said.

"I am acting my age and I'm not playing games."
She snapped, becoming defensive and she folded her arms
and took a step back. "I just feel like a conversation needs

to be had before we go any further. I don't want any drama with her over you. I have to work with her."

"So, what happens if she says she's not cool with you fuckin with me? What then? You gone choose her over your own happiness?"

She looked down at the floor. "I don't know, Dro. I just want to be on bad terms with her. I don't want y'all to be on bad terms. I just want peace."

"Iyanna, you worried about all the wrong stuff. If your last situation didn't teach you anything else. It should've taught you to put you first because everyone else will put themselves first. Fuck Keema! She's happy. I don't interfere with her personal life, and she doesn't interfere with mine. That woman was fuckin my cousin. Do you think she dropped by or sent a text to ask for my permission?" I didn't wait for a reply. "Fuck no, she didn't."

She looked torn.

"I'll tell you what. I'll make the decision. I'm done. If you need another woman to decide for you then you aren't the woman, I thought you were." I turned to walk away and felt her grab my arm.

"Dro wait! I don't want you to go. I really like you. I'm just saying that I don't want any drama."

𝕿

I snatched away. "Yeah, me either."

I walked over to the nightstand and grabbed my keys and walked out.

****

When I arrived at home, Juicy's car was in my driveway and she was walking down the steps but when she saw me, she stopped.

"Yo, today is not my fuckin day for real." I said, turning into the driveway. I parked and got out of the car. "Man, why the fuck are you at my house?"

"I want my money. I've been by here a few times, but you weren't home. I guess, that new bitch getting all of your time. You didn't want a girlfriend though." She said swiveling her chubby neck.

"Please get the fuck off my porch and out of my yard." I said, reaching in my pocket. I took out my wallet and thumbed through the bills and took out a twenty. "Here's your twenty dollars." I held it out. "Now, hopefully you will leave me the fuck alone and move on with your life."

She snatched the twenty from my hand, ripped it up, and then tossed it in my face. "I don't need your fuckin money!"

"Bitch, didn't you just say you wanted your money?" I asked, closing the space between us. I pressed my index finger against her forehead, giving it a hard shove. "I don't have time for this shit. I'm trying to be a better nigga than I was before but you about to make me beat your ass and catch a fuckin charge. Then I'll have to beat your fat ass again when I get out for making me fuck you up and be away from my son. Get the fuck out of my yard, Juicy!"

"Is that what makes that black bitch you fuckin better than me? Is it because she's smaller? Is that why you can be out in public parading that bitch around? Why couldn't I get that?" She screamed in my face, unfazed by my threats.

It dawned on me now that she was here because she'd seen me with Iyanna. "What you're stalking me now?"

"Fuck no! I ain't stalking your ass." She twisted up her face. "If you're out here parading her around of course I'm gonna see you. Don't we live in the same city nigga?"

I was tired of talking to her. "Man, just leave."

"Why? Is your bitch coming?" She asked, placing her hand on her hip. "I hope she does pull up. So, I can tell her what type of low-down nigga she's dealing with. I also want to tell her about the little gift we share." She smirked.

"Gift? What gift?" I asked, confused.

"Our little gift." She giggled.

"Man, I don't have time for your games. If you're implying that you're pregnant. I know that's a damn lie because you would've been announced that shit. So, try again." I told her. "Why won't you just go home? You are making yourself look real stupid."

"Naw, I made myself look stupid when I was fuckin with you!" She countered. "But it's all good. I ain't the only one who's gonna be looking stupid."

"Okay, Juicy." I replied, ignoring her threat. "Well, you ain't fuckin with me now. So go live your life and leave me the fuck alone. I haven't bothered you. So, why are you here fuckin with me?"

"Because you played with my feelings and then moved on to the next bitch like I never existed. How do you think that shit made me feel?"

"Apparently like a fuckin pyscho."

"So, this is funny to you? My feelings are a fuckin joke to you?" She pushed me in the chest.

"Juicy keep your hands off of me."

"Nigga you put your hands on me first!" She yelled as her eyes filled with tears and they began to roll down her cheeks. "I really liked you. I was good to you. You knew, I was feeling you. I never lied to you about how I felt. I was going out of my way doing little sweet shit for you and you let me until it wasn't convenient for you anymore. Then, you switched up."

"I never asked you to do shit for me and I never lied to you about what we were. I always told you the truth. I can't help that you assumed we would be more if you did extra shit. You were cool but I never saw you how you saw me. I'm sorry if I hurt you but that doesn't change how I felt then or now."

She began sobbing loudly. I rubbed my hands over my head, praying she would just leave. God must've heard my prayers because she turned and began walking towards her car. When she did. I turned and went inside. I tossed my keys on the coffee table and flopped down on the sofa, resting my head on the back of it. This had already been a long day and it was only a little past noon.

The sound of my car alarm blaring and glass breaking caused me to jump to my feet. I ran to the front door and snatched it open. This fat bitch had a bat knocking the windows out of my car.

"Oh hell naw!" I started out the door, but DJ popped in my head and I stopped on the porch. Taking my phone out, I dialed 9-1-1. "You might want to tape that twenty back together you wide back bitch because you're gonna need it for bail!" I yelled, just as the 9-1-1 dispatcher came on the line.

"9-1-1, what's your emergency?" A male voice came on the line.

"I need an officer at 27363 Burke Avenue. There's a crazy fat bitch here beating my fuckin car with a bat." I informed him.

"Sir, do you know the person that's vandalizing your property?" the dispatcher asked.

"Yes, her name is Jayel Smith."

"Okay, I'm sending a squad car to you now."

"You might want to send two. It's gonna take more than one to contain this psycho. I hope they have some bear mace or something. They may have to shoot this bitch and I promise I won't protest!"

"I don't give a fuck about no police! What you think, I'm gonna run?" Juicy roared as she continued her assault on my car. By now, her hair was all over her head and she was sweating profusely. She stopped hitting the car and started towards the porch.

I took the phone from my ear. "Now, if you bring your ass up here and hit me with that bat. I promise you, I'm going to take it and wear your ass out. So, for your safety. I suggest you stop while you're safe. You're already going to jail. Don't make them folks have to stop your ass by the ER first!" I warned.

"I ain't scared of you!" She replied but stopped walking.

I heard sirens blaring. "Thank goodness."

Just as the two squad cars pulled up next to the curb and parked. Juicy started running full speed towards the porch and up the steps. She swung the bat and hit me across the shoulder. I tried to snatch it, but she swung it again and hit me in the side of the head, dazing me. I stumbled backwards, shaking my head, trying to get myself together. The officers ran onto the porch, tackled Juicy to the ground, and placed the cuffs on her. Once she was cuffed, one of the officers came over to check on me.

"Sir, you're bleeding and that's a pretty nasty gash on the side of your head. You need medical attention. I'm going to call an ambulance for you." I heard him say but I was in so much pain that I couldn't respond.

"I hope you and your bitch enjoy them herpes mothafucka!" Juicy laughed, as she was being dragged down the steps. "That's right! I have herpes! Courtesy of the last fuck nigga I gave my heart too! I felt bad for knowingly giving it to you at first but not anymore! Itch itch mothafucka!"

Herpes? I knew, I'd fucked her raw a few times. So, I knew if she was telling the truth there was a possibility that I might have it but I hadn't experienced any symptoms. Maybe she was lying. *Please God, let her be lying. I swear, she'd better hope they keep her ass caged up because the next time I lay eyes on that bitch. I'm rockin her shit on sight! And if she gave me herpes, her ass is as good as dead! On God!*

Yaya

The weekend had dragged by after the blow up with Dro. I was worried about him because I hadn't heard anything from him. I'd tried calling and texting him but gotten no response. He hadn't been active on social media at all. So, I didn't know what to think. I knew he was upset with me but that didn't explain him just seemingly disappearing. I'd decided to stop trying to reach out to him and allow him time to cool off. Besides, right after he'd left my house, Mari had called and given me some devastating news. She'd told me that Choc's daughter had passed away due to being hit by a car and to my understanding both Brie and Choc were in jail. Mari had said that everyone was saying that Brie was at fault because she'd left their daughter at the playground while trying to get drugs and Choc had tried to choke Brie in front of the police. I can't say I blamed him because I would've done the same thing. I now felt guilty for how I'd treated him when he'd explained their situation to me. I'd really believed that he was lying and just wanted to be with Brie but now I realized that his children had really needed him. However, I still felt that he should've taken his children and left Brie because apparently, I'd been right about him not being able to help her. I hated that he was dealing with such a tragic loss. I wanted to be there for him, but I wasn't even sure if he wanted me to be after the way I'd treated him.

I walked into work Monday morning with a million and one thoughts running through my head. I was worried about both Choc and Dro. How had I managed to get myself in this situation? I'd gone from being heartbroken over Choc and wanting to get as far away from our situation as possible to finally meeting someone who took my mind off of him and made me feel special, but I'd ruined that. Now, here I was with no one and feeling guilty about both situations. I was literally caught in the middle of one of those urban fiction toxic love triangles that you read about.

"Good morning, Yaya." Judy greeted me as I walked in. "You're late. Is everything ok? I'm asking because you're normally one of the first people through the door. I was starting to get worried because I hadn't heard from you."

"Yeah, everything's fine." I lied, setting down my pocketbook and beginning to take my things out of my bag.

So, I could start on my client, who was seated in the waiting area waiting on me.

Judy came closer and whispered. "I heard about Choc's daughter. How is he?"

I looked up at her, my eyes instantly filling with tears. My heart hurt for Choc. I couldn't even begin to imagine how he must have felt but just knowing that he was hurting, hurt me. "I haven't talked to him." I admitted. I decided not to mention him being in jail because I didn't feel like it was my place to spread that. If she knew, she knew but she wouldn't be getting any information out of me.

Judy reached out touching my arm gently. "I apologize. I didn't mean to upset you. I just wanted to know how Choc was holding up. I know he must be devastated."

This was the only thing I hated about Judy. She never knew how to stop talking. Clearly talking about this was difficult for me and she'd literally just apologized but continued talking about it. "Judy, I don't want to talk about this, anymore. I need to get to my client."

An unreadable expression covered her face. "Oh my bad." She replied, walking away.

I finished setting up and then went to get my client.

I was halfway through retwisting my client's locs when Keema came over and flopped down in the empty styling chair next to me.

"Hey girl." She giggled, ripping open a bag of chips and stuffing a few in her mouth.

"Hey, Keema." I replied, somberly.

"Girl, why are you looking so sad?" She asked, with a smirk. Something in her tone wasn't right, almost like she was trying to be funny, but I was confused as to why she would find it funny that Choc's daughter had passed. I was sure that she'd heard, which was the reason behind her asking why I was looking sad.

"Keema, I'm not in the mood for you trying to be funny. I don't find anything funny about Choc's daughter passing. I know that's why you asked why I'm looking sad." I let her know, feeling myself on the brink of cussing her out. Somethings were simply off limits.

"Oooo, so you're upset for Choc. I wasn't sure which one of your men you were crying over being that they both had a shitty weekend." She laughed. "Then again, I'm sure you know my baby daddy was released from the hospital this morning. Chile, when I found out that crazy bitch had given him a concussion, I almost laughed myself to death. Karma is a bitch! Ain't it?"

214

I looked at her confused. How had she found out about Dro and I? And why had Dro been in the hospital? This explained why I hadn't heard from him.

Keema threw her head back erupting with laughter. "Why is your face like that? What's wrong stink? Let me guess, you've been counseling him on our coparenting relationship? Coaching him on how to express himself without the cursing or raising his voice."

"Keema, listen, this is not the time nor place for this. We are at work."

"I know where we are." She clarified.

"Nothing has happened between Dro and I, we are just friends. I told him that nothing could happen until I spoke with you. Our friendship is way more important than a man."

"Our friendship?" Keema laughed even louder. "Girl, what? Speak with me? On which night that he spent at your house did you tell him that? Are you serious right now?"

"Mmmph…" That was my client, Terry.

I let out a frustrated breath, trying to calm myself down. I hated it when someone tried to be funny with me in front of people. "Keema, we can talk about this another time but I'm not about to do this with you right now. I have a lot on my mind today and like I told you before, this isn't the time nor place." I tried to focus my attention back on Terry's hair but of course Keema wouldn't let it go.

"Nah there ain't nothing to talk about, sis. I ain't trippin bout Dro. You can have him. Shit, if you want, I'll make it a package deal. You can play step-mommy to DJ, too. I mean, since you and Dro both seem to have this parenting shit figured out and you said you wanted a baby with Choc. A chocolate baby, right? I mean, Choc already has a baby on the way, and he just lost one. So, I doubt if he wants another right away. He has a lot of shit going on at the moment. If you take my deal, you'll already have your own little premade family."

Something inside of me snapped. I let go of Terry's hair and was standing over Keema within a split second. "Bitch, I said today ain't the mothafuckin day! So, take your ass on somewhere!"

"Oh, you big mad, huh? Why are you so upset? You're fuckin my baby daddy. I ain't trippin. I just wanted to let you know, you don't have to be sneaky about it. You can be out in the open with your shit." Keema still continued to laugh, while sucking cheese from her fingers that had come off the chips she was eating. "One thing's for sure, you love the next bitch's baby daddy. I wish you had a baby daddy so I could fuck him, but I guess that old pussy doesn't get wet enough for a nigga to get you pregnant."

"That's enough!" Judy seemed to appear out of nowhere. She must've known shit was about to get ugly up in there. She stood between Keema and I. "I don't know what's going on and I don't care but this isn't the place for it."

"That's what I said but she wouldn't let it go." I snapped, my eyes still locked on Keema. She had me all the way fucked up and in that moment, I didn't care about my career or going to jail. I was ready to drag her ratchet ass. The audacity of her to come at me like this over a man she didn't even want had me hot. This bitch didn't even want her baby. So, why was she doing the most over Dro?

"Well, it's done now." Judy replied, looking back and forth between Keema and I. "Keema, go back to your station and stay over there."

"With all due respect, Judy. I'm grown and I can go anywhere in here I please. Ain't nobody gone do nothing to that sneaky hoe." Keema said, rolling her eyes while swiveling her neck.

"Hoe? Girl, you must be looking in the mirror. You stay fuckin and suckin a different nigga. You got some nerve calling somebody a hoe." I let her know.

Keema tossed the chip bag she'd been holding in my direction but it landed on the floor next to me. "Shut yo old ass up, HOE!"

"You'd better be glad that shit didn't hit me!" I warned.

"And if it had?" She challenged.

I opened my mouth to respond but Judy held up her hand to silence me. "Yaya get back to work!" She ordered, sternly. Then, looked back at Keema. "Gather your things and take the rest of the day off to get yourself together. If you can't come back tomorrow with a different attitude. Don't come."

"Why do I have to leave?" Keema wanted to know. She jumped to her feet, placing her hand on her small hip as she waited for a response from Judy.

"Because I said so." Judy replied, placing her hand on her hip as well, matching Keema's energy. "Go home Keema before you end up unemployed."

"This is some straight bullshit." Keema huffed, stomping off in the direction of her station.

"I apologize for this display of unprofessionalism." Judy spoke to Terry while cutting her eyes at me. "Come see me when you're done." With that she walked off.

"Terry give me a second. I need to use the restroom."

"Mmmhmmm." Was Terry's reply. I figured she felt some kind of way about me being late and me stopping on her hair to go back and forth with Keema but that hadn't been my fault. Still I felt the need to apologize. "I apologize for being so unprofessional and to make up for that. I'll give you a discount when we're done."

"Yeah, ok." Terry replied, taking out her phone and starting to fidget with it.

Instead, of saying anything about her rudeness, I went ahead to the bathroom. The last thing I needed was to get into it with a client as well. After going to the bathroom and pulling myself together. So, that I could focus. I went back out into the salon and got back to work on Terry's hair. A few minutes passed, before Terry decided to speak her mind.

"If that had been me. I would've whooped your ass and found another job because ain't no way a bitch gone play in my face like that and I let it slide."

"Excuse me?" I asked, looking at her through the mirror. I'd heard exactly what she'd said but I was confused as to why she'd felt the need to say it and I wanted her to say it again to be sure that I'd heard every word correctly before reacting.

She looked in the mirror, giving me a stank expression. "I said if that had been me, I would've whooped your ass."

I let go of her hair and spent the styling chair around so that she was facing me. I took a few steps back, extending my arms. "Well, pretend I'm fuckin your baby daddy and whoop it then bitch! Pretend I played in your face!"

Terry jumped to her feet, getting in my face. "Bitch, this ain't what you want!"

"Yes, the fuck it is!" I stood chest to chest with her.

Judy was back like The Flash! "Go home, Iyanna!" She demanded getting in between us. A few other stylists joined in, trying to defuse the situation. "I don't know what everyone's problem seems to be today but I'm not having that mess up in here! This is a salon not the hood!"

I grabbed my pocketbook and headed for the door, leaving everything else behind. As I was leaving, I heard Terry yell.

"I'll see you around bitch!"

I stopped walking and turned around. "You see me now hoe! Step outside!" I was fed up with people feeling as if they could say whatever they wanted to me. Those days of letting shit go in order to keep the peace was over for me.

"You're the hoe! Y'all nasty bitches love fucking behind the next bitch!"

"Girl, I ain't about to go back and forth with you. You've been to my house to get them straggly ass locs done before. Pull up! You know the address." With that I turned and left.

On my way home, I called Mari and Ajah and filled them in on what had just happened.

"Don't either of them hoes want no smoke." Ajah fumed. "Keema doing all of that over Dro when she's the biggest slut, I know."

"For real, though." Mari agreed. "And what the fuck does Terry have to do with it? I know her ass real good. Her husband ain't shit. He be fucking all them young girls and giving them money and shit. She needs to worry about her own miserable ass marriage and not about what you and Keema got going on."

"Yeah, because worrying about other people's shit is going to get her ass whooped." Ajah replied.

"I don't need either of y'all to fight my battles. I can handle it." I told them. "I just hate that shit happened at my job. I tried to tell Dro, Keema was gonna act a fool. I knew it."

"Well, if it were me, I'd give her ass a real reason to act a fool now. I'd be fuckin the hell out of Dro's fine ass!" Mari laughed.

"Bitch, you would've been fucked him before now. Stop lying!" Ajah laughed.

"Yeah, you're right." Mari continued laughing.

I shook my head. "How in the hell did I get myself in all this drama?"

"All of what drama?" Ajah wanted to know.

"All of what just happened."

"Girl, Keema is a child. If it was bothering her so bad. She should've been said something. She said she knew about him spending the night at your house. She should've pulled up when she saw him there. She just wanted to approach you while she had an audience because hoes like her live for attention." Ajah explained.

"Exactly." Mari chimed in. "She could've also called you outside and spoke to you about it. She knew what she was doing. Like Ajah said she loves attention. She probably didn't think you were gonna say anything back to her. She knows you don't like confrontation."

"Yeah, well I fooled her ass today." I said, pulling into my driveway.

"Sis, don't let that shit bother you. Keema and Terry both will be alright as long as they don't touch you." Mari said.

"That part!" Ajah added.

"Yeah, I ain't worried about either of them." I let them know because I truly wasn't, but I knew regardless to what I said they would both go to war behind me without hesitation. Letting out a sigh, I said. "It's been a long morning and all this chaos has given me a headache. So, I'm going in here, take something, and lie down for a while."

"Okay, well call us back later." Ajah said.

"Okay. I will." I promised and then ended the call. I grabbed my pocketbook and went inside.

No sooner than I got inside, my cell began ringing. I looked down at the screen and saw Dro's name flashing on it. More than happy to hear from him, I hurriedly answered.

"Hello."

"What in the fuck is going on with you and Keema? She called me going off about she was gonna beat your ass and you tried to get her fired or some shit like that." Dro blurted, without even speaking.

"She said what?" I asked, not really asking but out of shock of how Keema had gone back and lied to him. "That girl is lying her tail off! She came into work and confronted me about us. I kept telling her, I didn't want to talk about it there and that we could talk later but you know how she is. She loves to show off in front of people. So, she wouldn't let the issue go until I'd had enough of her mouth and was ready to punch her in it. So, the boss told her to go home."

I heard him let out a frustrated breath. "I knew that bird was lying. The shit she was saying didn't even sound right."

Even though, Keema and I were on bad terms. It bothered me to hear him refer to her as a bird but I didn't speak on it. "Yeah, she's definitely lying." I shook my head and then asked. "How are you feeling? Keema mentioned something about some girl giving you a concussion and you being in the hospital. What happened?"

"I bet she did. That's why I don't fuck with her like that. She couldn't wait to spread that. She's so fuckin miserable. It makes her happy to know that I'm hurt in anyway." He explained. "Yeah, this crazy chick I used to fuck with showed up at my house on some crazy shit. Long story short, she fucked up my car with a bat and then hit me

224

in the head with it but her ass is in jail now. Well, I guess she's in jail. I pray for her safety that she's in jail because if I see her. Her ass is mine."

"Naw, don't go getting yourself in trouble. Let the police handle her." I told him.

"No disrespect but that situation has nothing to do with you and I plan on handling it however I see fit." He let me know. "I really didn't call to talk about that, though. I didn't like how things went down between us the last time I saw you. I apologize for how I acted. I really didn't think Keema would be on no bullshit about us. Honestly, I really don't believe she cares at all. Like you said, she loves to show her ass. She's a drama queen."

"I agree with you there but I'm not stressing that mess. We're good as far as I'm concerned."

"I'm glad to hear that because I would love to continue getting to know you."

"I would like that too."

A smile spread across my lips. "Well, I'm glad we got that out the way."

"Me too." He replied. "So, can I see you later on?"

"Yeah, I'll be home."

"Okay. I'll stop by later. I have a few things to take care of first."

"Okay. I'm gonna take a nap. I have a headache."

"Do you have something to take for it?"

"Yeah."

"Good. Well, don't worry about cooking tonight. I'm going to bring by some food when I come."

"Sounds good to me."

"Aight…bet." With that he hung up and so did I.

After taking some Excedrin migraine, I grabbed a blanket and laid down on the sofa. It wasn't long before sleep consumed me.

****

I was awakened by the ringing of the doorbell.

"I'm coming." I mumbled, sitting up on the sofa, trying to gather my thoughts and remember where I was. The room was completely dark. Whoever was at the door continued to ring the bell. "I'm coming!" I repeated, louder this time. Finally, it came to me that Dro was supposed to be stopping by. I tossed the blanket back and got up, stumbling over my shoes that I'd left next to the sofa. "Shit!"

When I reached the door, I turned on the porch light. Then unlocked the door and swung it open. "My bad, I'd..." my words trailed off when my eyes met Choc's. He looked drained. I could tell Jada's death was weighing heavily on him.

"Can I come in?" He asked, his voice was hoarse.

"Yeah...of course." I replied, stepping back out of the way to let him in. Seeing him like this tugged at my heart.

He walked in past me, into the living room. I closed the door and followed him. Walking over to the lamp in the corner, I turned it on.

"Have a seat." I offered. "I'll be right back. I need to go wash my face. I just woke up."

"That's cool. Go on and handle your business." He said, taking a seat on the sofa.

I went down the hall to the bathroom, washed my face, and brushed my teeth. When I was done, I returned to the living room where Choc was waiting. I could see the pain etched all over his face. I took a seat at the end of the sofa, not sure of what to say. So, I said the only thing I knew to say in a situation like this.

"I'm sorry to hear about Jada. I can't imagine what you must be going through."

Choc ran his hand over his face before replying. "Yeah, this shit's crazy. I still can't believe it."

I saw tears pooling in his eyes and moved down next to him on the sofa. I reached over and placed my hand over his, giving it a light squeeze. "I know. I wish there was something I could do to take away your pain or change what has happened, but I know there's nothing I can do."

"There's nothing anyone can do." He replied, barely above a whisper. By now, tears were flowing down his cheeks. "I just want my baby back."

"I know you do." I whispered. I moved closer and wrapped my arm around him. He laid his head on my chest and broke down, sobbing like a baby. I wrapped my other arm around him, rocking him back and forth. By now, I too was crying. "It's gonna be ok, baby. I got you." I told him and I meant it. In this moment, Brie or Dro didn't exist. The only people that mattered was us. He needed me and I planned to stand beside him. I didn't care about anything that had happened. None of that mattered. What mattered was the man I loved with all my heart was hurting and needed me. It was crazy how in an instant my feelings for him all came rushing back. I don't know what it was that made me still love him this way after all that had happened but I did. I loved him so much. As I sat here holding him, I selfishly began dreaming about the future. Brie was gone. I didn't have to worry about him ever forgiving her and if I road this thing out with him. I knew, he would forever be grateful. He would finally see that I was truly the one. He would see what I'd been trying to prove to him forever. My love for him ran deep and it was unconditional. My thoughts got carried away and I began to dream about giving him a daughter, not to replace Jada because I knew that wasn't possible but to help fill the void of losing her and to also have what I'd wanted for years. I wanted us to get custody of Justice and the new baby and be one big happy family. My heart swelled at the thought of it.

"I'm sorry for coming here and breaking down like this." Choc spoke, interrupting my thoughts. His head still resting on my chest. "I didn't know where else to go. This was the only place that felt right."

"You did right. Don't apologize. I'm glad you're here. I was worried about you but I wasn't sure if you wanted to hear from me after how I'd treated you." I confessed, rubbing his back.

Choc sat up and looked at me. Reaching out, he caressed the side of my face. "Of course, I wanted to hear from you. As crazy as it may sound, after finding out about Jada, you were the first person to come to mind. If I'd chosen, you instead of Brie none of this shit would've happened." He dropped his head, shaking it back and forth. "I fucked up, Yaya."

"It's ok, baby. You didn't know things would turn out this way."

"I knew, she was fucked up. I should've left and taken my kids. She needed more help than I could provide or anyone else for that matter. I knew that!" He screamed, jumping to his feet. He started pacing back and forth.

I got up and walked over to him. "You can't blame yourself." I told him.

"Who the fuck else is to blame?"

"Brie! That's who! She should've fought harder to beat her addiction. No one could've helped her until she was willing to help herself. That's not on you or her parents. That's on her." I preached.

"Naw, I didn't protect my babies. That shit is on me." He disagreed.

I knew there was no convincing him otherwise tonight. So, I decided to let it go. "Have you eaten?"

"I'm not hungry. I just need something for this headache and to lie down for a minute. Once this headache eases up. I'll get out of your hair. Grandma Lizzie said I could stay at her place for the time being because I can't go back to that apartment."

"You can stay here." The words slipped from my lips without hesitation. I didn't want him to go. I finally had him back and I didn't want him out of my sight.

He looked shocked. "Here? Are you sure? I mean, I know…"

I placed my hand over his lips. "I'm sure."

He reached up and took my hand, kissing it. "I love you, Ya. Thank you."

Out of nowhere, images of our last morning together flashed through my head. I remembered him saying the same thing before he'd walked out and chosen Brie over me. I shook my head, trying to shake the images away in hopes that the feeling that had invaded the pit of my stomach and my chest would also go away. The pain that I'd felt after learning the truth about why he'd been so adamant about me knowing he loved me, returned. Almost knocking the breath out of me. Tears filled my eyes, again.

"What's wrong?" Choc asked, a concerned expression taking over his face.

"Nothing." I lied, shaking my head. "I love you, too."

He pulled me to him and wrapped his arms around me, tightly. "I know a lot of shit has happened and I still have a lot going on, but I need you so much right now."

"I know you do." I replied, wrapping my arms around him. "I got you."

"Thank you."

I was the first to pull away. "Come on, let's get you something to take for that headache."

"Okay."

We went into the kitchen, and I gave him two Excedrin from the bottle that I'd left on the counter earlier and a glass of water. When he was done taking the Excedrin, we went down the hall to the bedroom and he undressed down to his boxers and got in the bed. I turned off the light for him and went back down the hall to the living room. I thought about calling Ajah and Mari, but I didn't feel like getting a speech from them about allowing Choc to stay. So, I decided to wait on calling them. My mind went to Dro. I needed to cancel our plans. I picked up my cell from the coffee table and at the same time the doorbell rang. My heart began beating rapidly against my chest. "Shit!" I said, jumping to my feet. I rushed to the door, not wanting Choc to come down the hall. I opened the door and slipped out onto the porch, closing it behind me.

"Hey, beautiful." Dro smiled, holding flowers in one hand and a bag of Chinese in the other.

Dro

Yaya opened the door and stepped outside onto the porch, closing the door behind her. I found that to be strange but I didn't question it. "Hello, beautiful." I greeted her.

"H-hey, Dro." She spoke, her eyes roaming around nervously.

"What's up? Is everything ok? You seem nervous. What's going on?" I wanted to know.

"Yeah, everything's fine." Her eyes finally found mine but only for a second before she diverted them in the other direction. "I know, I said that we could have dinner tonight, but something came up and I was hoping that we could cancel and get together some other time."

Confused as to why she would wait till I bought food and drove all the way to her house. I couldn't help but ask. "Iyanna, what's really going on? You know, I'm not the type of nigga for games. So just keep it a band with me. We made plans hours ago. You had plenty of time to cancel. So, what just so happened to come up as soon as I arrived?"

"Ummm…well…it didn't…" The door opened and Choc stepped out onto the porch. "Ya, what you got going on?" He looked from her to me then back at her. "Do you need me to leave? So you can entertain ya man?"

"No, you don't have to leave." She hurriedly answered. "Can you just give us a minute?"

"Yeah." He snapped, mean mugging me. Before, going back inside.

"Yo, I'm bout to slide." I said, holding out the flowers and food. "You can keep this shit. I don't have time for this. I see what time it is."

Taking the food and flowers from my hand, she put everything on the porch and reached out grabbing my hand. "Dro, it's not what you think. He just lost his daughter and needed a place to stay for a few days. He didn't have anywhere else to go. I'm just trying to be here for him."

I snatched my hand out of her grasp. "That's bullshit and you know it. That nigga got family. You probably volunteered your help."

"I did but…"

"But my ass! I don't have time for games. If you want that nigga then be woman enough to admit it yo me. Don't stand in my face and act like you're just being a Good Samaritan. We both know what time it is." I told her. "You think being here for him in his time of need is gonna change him but it won't. If that nigga did you dirty before he will do it again. When I met you. You were sick behind how he'd left you for his baby mama. Over the past few weeks, I've been the nigga here putting a smile on your face, trying to show you that you deserve better than being a nigga's second chance but I can see that you like being a second choice. If this shit hadn't happened, he would still be over there with his family. He's only here now because plan A didn't work out. I guess, he always has plan B though."

"Dro, you don't know the whole story! So, stop speaking on shit you know nothing about." She snapped. I saw anger dancing in her brown eyes.

"You're right I don't know the full story. I only know what you told me. That nigga dropped you and went back to his baby mama."

"You know what? I don't have time for this shit. Get the fuck off my porch before you end up with another bandage." She retorted coldly.

"Bit...Iyanna, trust me you ain't built like that because the next bitch that puts her hands on me will be wearing a matching bandage and that's on my son." I let her know, in the same cold tone. Looking her up and down, shook my head. "And here I was thinking you were different...smarter. You're just another goofy ass broad who enjoys being dragged by a nigga then sit up somewhere crying about how you've been done wrong. That's what you deserve." With that I turned and started down the steps.

"Fuck you, Dro. Keema was right. You think you know every fuckin thing and don't know shit. With your judgmental ass. Obviously, you ain't the best at decisions making when it comes to relationships. You have a ratchet ass baby mama that doesn't want her son and crazy bitches bussin your head open for fun! Sweep around your own front door before you go judging mine!"

"Girl, fuck you!" I didn't even stop or turn around. I just continued to my rental, got inside, and left.

THANK YOU'S

First and foremost, I would like to thank God for everything. Without him nothing would be possible. I thank him for blessing me with this wonderful gift to be able to write and entertain people with my stories. Secondly, I would like to thank my three beautiful babies, Ny'Ajah, Camari, and AnTeyvion. You three are the reason that I grind so hard and continue to strive for more and to become a better me. Times when I feel like giving up, I know I can't because of you three (even though you're all grown lol). I would like to thank my mom, Angela Taylor (R.I.P) and my dad, Paul Hill. I am thankful for and appreciate you both. To my grandmothers Ann West (R.I.P) and Mable Hill (R.I.P), I love you both and thank you for being there for me whenever I have ever needed you. To my sister and my best friend Tinika Taylor, I love you more than life itself. You are my rock, the one person I can depend on when everyone else in this harsh world has turned their backs on me! I treasure every moment the two of us spend together. Also, thank you for pushing me to write, again. You stayed on me until I got back at it! Thank you! Thank you! Thank you! Thank you! To my friend, Kimberly Rawlings, girl we have come a long way. I appreciate you for being with me through all my drama lol. For real, I can always count on you when I need you and that means a lot.

To all of my aunts, uncles and cousins, I love you guys. R.I.P to my uncles Steve and Calvin, I miss you both very much. A special shout out to my uncle Al Kelly, even though we don't get to see each other much anymore because of our hectic schedules, I love you to pieces and thank you so much for the love and support that you have shown me.

A huge thanks to my bestie, who is like a second mom, Delores Miles. Thanks for always being here for me whenever I call. I love you to pieces.

Now I'd like to thank all of the readers who follow my work! Thank you to each one of you, who has ever purchased any of my work or just taken time to read an excerpt of mine. I appreciate it.

Thank you to Cash who has believed in a sista since day one. I can't begin to express to you how much your friendship and constant advice and support means to me. I love you and will always treasure our friendship.

If I have forgotten anyone I truly apologize. I suck at this lol. Please know that it wasn't intentional.

Made in the USA
Middletown, DE
05 July 2023

34598443R00136